WINDRIDER
FORBIDDEN FLIGHT

H.G. CHAMBERS

Copyright ©2019 H.G. Chambers
All rights reserved. This book or any portion thereof may not be reproduced or used in any manner whatsoever without the express written permission of the publisher except for the use of brief quotations in a book review.

First Printing, 2018
Editing: Jane Tucker
Cover Design: www.vividcovers.com

https://hgchambers.com

Books by H.G. Chambers

WINDWALKER SERIES

Windwalker: Forbidden Flight

Windwalker: Relic of the Dead

THE AETERNUM CHRONICLES

Recreance (Book 1)

Vigilance (Book 2)

Defiance (Book 3)

For you, Mom.

CONTENTS

Keep Dreaming................................. 7
The Proving Ceremony 25
Trials.. 31
Windfaith 42
Out and Up 56
Jonah 64
Rüh... 72
First Flight...................................... 81
The Harab Maneuver 89
Skyhunter.. 110
Mehalia 121
The Bonding 131
The Trial... 143
Temperance..................................... 147
Exile 163
The Storm 177
Protection 189
Exultation 194
Extras... 208
Acknowledgments 221
Newsletter 222

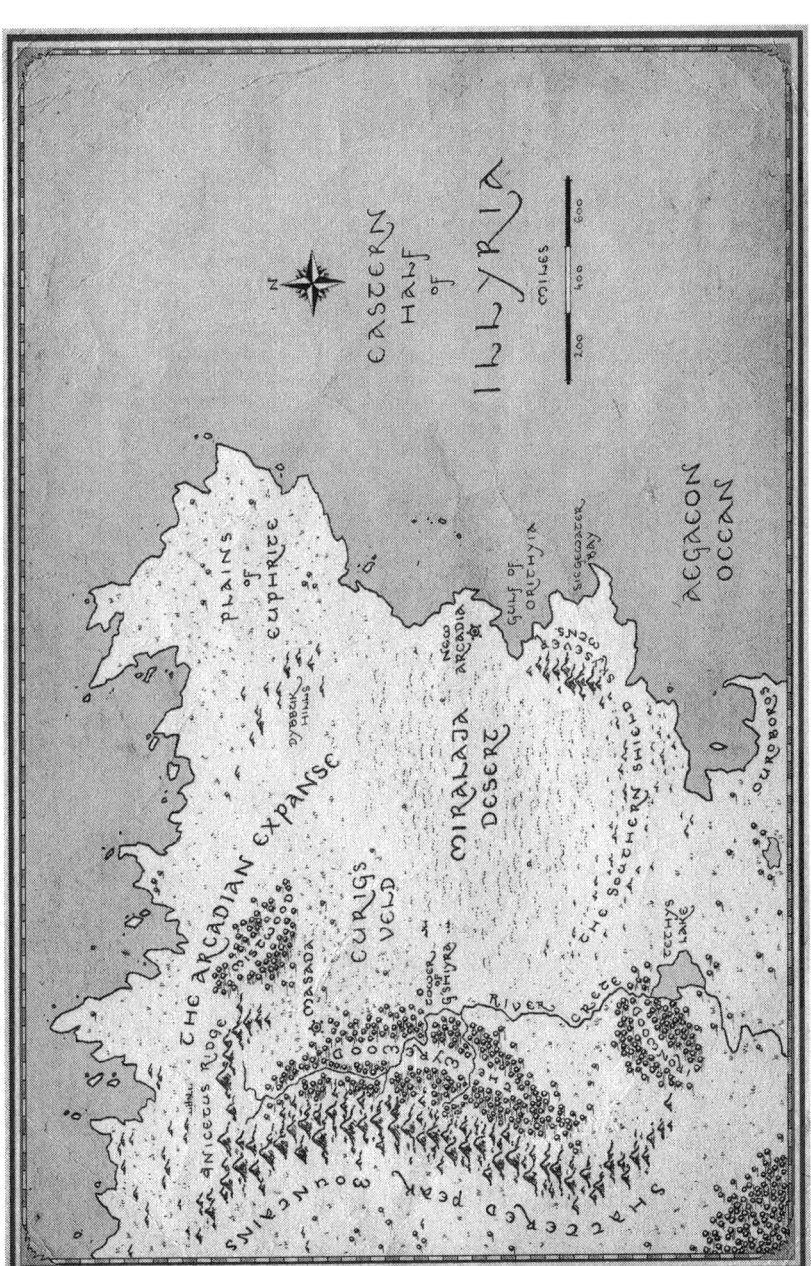

Surrounded by towering walls of flat-topped mesas, an enduring civilization of desert people known as the Sahra' make their homes amid the sand and stone of the Miralaja desert.

KEEP DREAMING

Kivanya Fariq clung to the sheer rock face of the towering desert butte. The sun beat down relentlessly, drawing beads of moisture from her forehead. No encumbering ropes or harnesses tethered her to the craggy surface—she held on by the strength of her practiced fingers, and her will to live. There was no time to worry about the cracked, sandy hardpan hundreds of feet below. She was focused on one thing: reaching the top as quickly as possible.

Kivanya—or Kiva, as she would have it—wedged the fingers of her left hand into a vertical crack. Her feet were crowded onto a narrow ledge, and her right hand was open, poised to grasp a handhold three paces overhead.

She vaulted up toward her target, but as she did the stone beneath her feet crumbled. Kiva's heart dropped as her fingertips grazed the handhold, failing to gain purchase. She swung out, hanging by four of the five fingers on her left hand. Below, the loose stone tumbled away, a large chunk of which careened along the rocky face of the butte, eventually smashing into a thousand pieces on the desert floor.

Kiva grit her teeth and shifted her weight. She used her legs to swing sideways, reaching for a suitable crag with her right hand. She caught and wedged her fingers into the small space. With both hands secured and her feet resting against the stone, Kiva scanned for the competition.

"*Al'ama*," she cursed. Kiva had been in the lead, but her brother Amir was now several paces higher. Oh no you don't, she thought, continuing her climb upon the face of the dusty, reddish-brown rock.

He paused, grinning down at her. "Watch your grip, tifl!"

At seventeen years old, Amir was just one year older than she was, and in no position to be calling her *child*.

"I'll show you who's the tifl," she muttered, digging her toes into a crevice and vaulting upward. Her hands found the inside of a long diagonal crack, and she began inching her way up it.

Amir, realizing his lead was in jeopardy, quickly resumed his climb.

The sun was well on its westward journey, yet still strong enough to warm the breeze. Kiva used her shoulder to wipe the sweat from her brow, then pulled herself up into a large rock cleft with vertical parallel sides. The cleft was wide enough for her to fit inside, but narrow enough that she could use her back and feet to apply opposite pressure on the walls. She quickly progressed up the cleft, then pulled herself onto a small, flat shelf at its top.

Kiva again looked for her brother, and this time smiled when she found him. Amir was directly across from her, struggling to find his next handhold on the sheer rock face.

Looking up, she could see a clear path to the butte's surface. This race belonged to her.

Ever since the beginning of the last windy season, Kiva

had begun to win these competitions against her brother. Still, Amir beat her as often as she won. *This will not be one of those times,* she told herself.

She continued scaling the varied stone, making her way toward the flat surface above. There was a scrabbling of rocks to her right, and her eyes widened in shock. Amir was scrambling up a narrow vertical crack, right past her.

"Hey!" she cried, doubling her efforts to stay ahead of him.

Side by side, they wrenched, leapt, and pulled their bodies over the stone surface.

Almost there!

Kiva reached up for the next handhold—the last one before the top—when she heard the slap of a hand on flat stone. "I win!" Amir shouted.

Kiva ignored him and continued climbing, pulling herself up onto the surface of the tabletop butte. Once clear of the edge, she lay on her back, panting.

Amir feigned a yawn, and Kiva sat up to glare at him. He sat on the edge, leaning back on his hands with his feet dangling over the drop.

Amir stood and walked over to where Kiva now sat, and pushed back the white shemagh cloth that had been covering his head. His dark hair was pulled back, tied loosely at the nape of his neck. He grinned broadly. Kiva would have smacked the grin off his face, had she not been so exhausted from the climb.

"I hope you don't mind, *Kivanya*, I've been saving my washing for weeks in preparation for just such a day as this one. I am sure that the extra scrubbing will help improve your hand strength," he taunted.

"It's *Kiva*," she growled, baring her teeth. She hated being called by her full name, and he knew it.

"Not so fast," their older brother spoke from behind.

Kiva turned to face him. Mica sat cross-legged, chewing on dunegrass as if he just happened to be there. The truth was, Mica was a better climber than either of them, and had reached the top well before. His long black hair was shaved on the sides, tied with a cord at the back. It was the traditional style of those affirmed in the sect of zilsiad—the shadestalkers.

"What do you mean, 'not so fast'?" Amir asked, crossing his arms.

"First to arrive atop the butte—this was the wager?" Mica asked casually.

"It was, and I arrived before Kiva," Amir insisted.

"Mhmm," Mica said, thoughtfully.

"What? We all saw that I was the first, clear as day."

"I saw that nearly thirty percent of you still dangled over the edge, at the time Kiva cleared it."

"But I was—"

"Technically, you hadn't *arrived* at the top. At least not all of you." Mica spoke it as if it were the most obvious thing in the world.

Kiva smiled. She knew Amir would not go against his older brother, even if he didn't think it was fair. As the eldest of the three, Mica had the final say. Kiva didn't care that it was a technicality. She'd take the win any way she could.

"This is ridiculous. Clearly I was the first one to reach the top. Why must you always take her side?" Amir griped.

Mica was two years his senior, and three to Kiva. Being the firstborn meant he got to do everything first. It also meant that he was faster, stronger, and more experienced at it. Granted, the same held true when comparing him to his peers. Kiva loved both her brothers, but she was especially fond of Mica.

She stood and patted Amir on the back. "Don't worry brother. *I've* only been saving my washing for *two* weeks. I'm sure you'll have no trouble getting the mud stains out with those big, strong hands of yours." She grinned mercilessly. Amir glowered at her, his pale blue eyes narrowing to slits.

"We should get back," Mica said. "Mother will be—"

He was cut off by a screech from overhead. All three of them looked up. A dark shape soared high above, in stark contrast with the expansive pale blue sky. It glided on the wind with its long neck outstretched. Its great wings and feathered hind legs were spread wide, providing a broad surface to catch the rising air. Trailing behind was a long black tail fanned out at the tip. On this wondrous predator's back, lying nearly prone, was a windwalker.

The three of them stood in silence for a moment, watching as its shadow sped over the surface of the butte, then raced out across the desert hardpan.

After a moment, Mica turned to Amir and spoke, "When will you make your challenge, brother?"

"Soon," he answered. "Maybe this year."

"Perhaps I will as well," said Kiva. She was still looking out toward the kiraeen and its rider. *What must it be like to soar on the wind?* She yearned in her heart of hearts to fly, though she feared it could never be, given who and what she was.

"Keep dreaming, Kiva," said Amir. "They'd never allow a girl windwalker, and even if by some miracle they did, any kiraeen you tried to bond would tear out your throat before you could blink."

Kiva ignored him. Her attention was on the windwalker and its kiraeen far above. She watched as they became nothing more than a small speck on the horizon.

"You'd be better off waiting a year or two," Mica advised her. "Believe me, once the mentors get a hold of you, they tend to not let go. Enjoy your youth while you still can."

Kiva sighed and said nothing. They were nearing the end of the withering season, which meant the proving ceremony was right around the corner. It had been two years since Mica issued his own challenge to the shadestalker sect, and won.

"Let's go," Mica said, turning to face Amir. "You'll want to get a good night's sleep, should you decide to challenge at the ceremony tomorrow."

They slid down the far side of the butte—which was sloped far more gradually than the side they climbed—and jogged toward the village. Along the way, something caught Kiva's eye, and she called for a stop. She scanned, looking for a pattern; something that didn't quite fit with the landscape.

"Will you come on? There's nothing there," Amir insisted.

"*Shh!*" Kiva hissed, furrowing her brow for one last look. *There!*

She'd spotted it. A pattern of gray-blue scales that blended almost perfectly with the faded scrag of a bush several feet away. She crept toward it slowly, her bare feet stepping silently across the thin layer of sand covering rocky ground. At twelve paces away she could see it clearly—a thick blue lizard the length of her arm-span, cooling itself under the wiry shrub.

Kiva made a clicking sound with her tongue, and snapped her fingers twice, placing them low to the ground. The lizard's head twitched, as it turned one of its eyes toward her.

She slowly placed her palm to the sand, and began rubbing it in a circular motion. The rhythmic sound it created was almost musical. She clicked her tongue again, and snapped with her free hand. The lizard slithered out toward her, stopping half way.

"Taealaa li, hubun," she coaxed, continuing to rub her hand in circles. The lizard raised its belly up, extending its short legs, and began moving toward her, its steps matching the rhythm of her hand on the sand.

Almost.

It drew closer, broad head weaving back and forth. Kiva reached back with her free hand, ever so slowly. Her fingers came upon the khanjar dagger sheathed at her silk belt, and she gently drew it out. The lizard was now an arm's length away. It paused, as if some ancient instinct were trying to warn it—death awaits down this path. But soon the rhythm of Kiva's hand in the sand erased its apprehension, and it again continued forward.

It took one more step, and with lightning speed, Kiva brought her blade down through the center of its head.

She grinned, holding up the dead lizard by the hilt of her dagger.

"Excellent catch, Kiva!" Mica nodded respectfully.

"I will never get used to how you do that," Amir said, shaking his head. Kiva glimpsed a ghost of a smile on his face.

She'd given them all good reason to be happy. Samin lizards were extremely rare, *and* exceptionally delicious…especially after nearly an entire season of boiled roots.

They continued their trek home, and after an hour at a quick pace, arrived at the walls of a massive, red stone mesa. To anyone who wasn't Sahra', the rock formations would appear as nothing more than enormous, barren obstacles to travel around. But inside they held a great secret.

Kiva, Amir, and Mica leapt from rock to rock, ascending to a hidden, shadowy vertical crack in the striated stone. They entered it single file, and continued along the narrow, winding path. Occasional shafts of sunlight broke through gaps in the stone above, until they traveled deeper in, and the walls on either side became cool to the touch. Kiva took a deep breath, enjoying the feeling of sweat cooling on her forehead.

They reached the end of the passage, and stepped out into the wide open bustling marketplace of Madina Basin. Kiva took in the sight of the hidden Sahra' city, gazing up at the towering walls of natural stone. These geological defenses surrounded the entire basin, providing it both concealment and physical protection from the outside world. High above, embedded into the upper portion of the walls were enormous sheets of rusted steel. They were hundreds of feet tall, curving slightly inward toward the top, and ending just before the walls did. *Sandsheilds,* Kiva recalled.

They were relics from a time long past, when sandstorms

grew so large that the walls alone were not enough to keep them out. Without the sandshields as evidence, Kiva wouldn't have believed such storms possible. Afternoon sunlight glinted off a great iron bell in a recessed niche beneath the sandshields—another relic of the past. The warning bell hadn't been rung in Kiva's lifetime, or her parents'.

There were no buildings in Madina Basin that hadn't been carved directly from the surrounding stone. Sahra' homes were dug out from great stepped layers of rock, stacked on top of each other and climbing upwards, like stairs fit for a giant. Hundreds of openings stared out from each step, each marking the entrance to a family abode. Madina Basin sheltered thousands of Sahra', and had done so for over one thousand years.

The great basin was bustling, filled with people out performing evening chores, bartering at the markets, and heading home from their sect halls. Over the din of the crowds, Kiva could hear the calls of the merchants, shouting the quality of their wares. Things here were the same as they'd been for hundreds of years, and all of it happening within the protective walls of the basin.

"*Girl!*" A gnarled old man was eying the dead lizard draped over her shoulders. "I'll give you two clay shakh pots for that mangy samin."

"Mangy?" she asked, incredulous.

"Yes! Mangy! If a twiggy girl like you can shoulder the scrawny thing, it *must* weigh next to nothing. Two pots!"

She took a step toward him, scowling. "Listen to me you bedraggled *qadim*—"

"*Thank you*," Mica interrupted with a smile, "but the samin is not for sale." He gently directed Kiva away.

"Your loss!" the man called out, before melting back into the crowd.

Mica gave her a look, and Kiva shrugged. "What?" she asked innocently. "He called me *twiggy!*"

"Come on!" Amir called. "I want a rematch. Last one home does the dishes!" He bolted off before either of them could stop him.

"Hey!" Kiva called, chasing after him. "Not fair! I've got an—*oof!*"

"*Ya wati!* Watch where you're going!" a woman's voice called from behind.

"Sorry!" she called back, running as quickly as she could given the thirty-five pound lizard on her shoulders.

By the time she reached her family's abode, she was drenched in a fresh layer of sweat, and her left shoulder was stained with dried lizard blood. The woven carpets that had been hanging outside were no longer there, which meant only one thing. Her mother was home.

"*Al'ama.*" Kiva cursed. She crept inside her family's dimly lit home, its high ceilings decorated with water inspired patterns of opal and glass shards. Despite the modest opening leading inside, the abode itself was rather spacious and cozy.

"Kivanya Raisel Fariq!"

Kiva ducked her head as her mother's voice stopped her in her tracks.

"If you get one drop of blood on my freshly cleaned rugs, *you* will be the one re-cleaning them…*all of them.*"

"Yes mama," she said quietly, turning toward the kitchen.

"Not so fast. Where were you this afternoon? You *knew* we were to visit the weavers hall today. I specifically told Lalla Netaniah that you would be present. How do you think that makes me look, when you run off like that!"

"Sorry mama, I—"

"Is that a rip in your tunic? Have you been climbing with your brothers again?"

"I—"

"*Enough!* I don't want to hear it. Take that mess of a samin to the cold room and dress it. I expect to see you at dinner, without the blood and dust."

Kiva pursed her lips. She knew if she tried to speak again her mother would cut her off, but she could not go until dismissed.

"Snake bite your tongue, girl? *Go!*" she yelled, pointing toward the kitchen.

Kiva could hear her mother mumbling under her breath as she fled into the kitchen.

Once there, Kiva set down the samin lizard and lit a small oil lamp, then lifted the handle on the wooden trap-door in the floor. She threw the lizard over her shoulder and climbed down into the cold room.

By the time she had finished dressing it and cleaning herself up, dinner was ready, and her mother was handing her dishes to bring to the dining table. She arrived in the dining room to find her father, Mica, and Amir already seated, sipping hot tea.

"Kivanya! Little moon, how was your day?" Kiva's father

asked, sitting cross-legged on a cushion at the head of the low dining table. He looked at her fondly with eyes of deep hazel, mingled with thin spikes of green extending from his pupils. His thickly muscled arms—earned through years of hard work in the stonemelter forges—rested at his sides with his hands upon his knees. At first glance, her father could easily be mistaken for a fearsome and imposing individual—a force to be reckoned with. But Kiva and her family knew the gentle truth of his soul. Haruk Fariq was slow to anger, and quick to forgive.

Kiva set down the lidded dishes and greeted her smiling father. "Hi Papa...My day was mundane and tedious, as usual," she said, hoping her mother hadn't told him of her transgressions.

"Is that so?" he asked. "Perhaps if you had gone to the weavers hall, it would have been more exciting," he said with a knowing smile.

Mica stifled a laugh.

Kiva forced a grin, pleading for mercy with her eyes.

"Though I'm sure your mother has already suggested it," he finished, taking a sip of tea.

She breathed a sigh of relief, grateful that she wouldn't be hearing it from him as well.

Her mother brought in the rest of the meal and they all began to dine on baked scorpion medallions, warm chava bread, and purple slices of boiled kerava root.

"Amir," her father asked, "have you decided whether you will be issuing a challenge at the ceremony tomorrow?"

Amir choked on his drink. He cleared his throat and answered, "I have not yet decided."

"You know, your brother was your age when he—"

"Issued his challenge for the zilsiad," Amir interrupted, gesturing dramatically. "The Sahra's greatest and most esteemed battle sect. Yes, I know."

There was a long moment of awkward silence before Amir sighed and spoke again, "Sorry. I'm just…it's just nerves. I want to challenge, I'm just not sure if I'm ready."

"No one ever feels ready," Mica said.

"But what if I fail? All of the training will have been for nothing." Amir was looking at his father. He had spent the past three years apprenticing with him in the forges, helping to craft weapons for the warrior sects. They all knew Amir would at some point be issuing a challenge for the stonemelter sect. It was just a matter of when. Challenging too early could mean failure, and once a challenge is failed, the door to that sect is closed, forever.

"Easy. You pick another sect," Kiva said, earning a glare from her mother.

"What?" Kiva asked, eyebrows raised. "It's true…"

"Look at me, son," their father said, setting down his bread. "You have worked *hard* over the past three years. I've seen you craft steel worthy of the stonemelters fifty times over. Should you choose this year as your proving, you will succeed."

Amir sat silently for a moment, staring down at the half-eaten food on his plate. The tension hung in the air, as everyone waited for his reaction, except Kiva, who casually shoved three scorpion medallions in her mouth and drank deeply from her cup.

Right when it seemed he'd not say anything at all, Amir

finally spoke, "Alright. Tomorrow, then. I will issue my challenge tomorrow."

The table erupted with cheers. Mica and their father stood and slapped Amir on the back, congratulating him, while their mother rushed to the kitchen. She returned a moment later, her face aglow, holding a tray with a fresh pitcher of jallab and five cups.

"We are *so* proud of you, son," she said, setting down the tray. She grasped his face in both hands and kissed the top of his head. "I know you will succeed."

"Thank you, Mama," he said, smiling nervously.

"We will *all* be there to support you," she said, with a stern glance at her daughter. The look wasn't unjustified. Kiva had nearly missed Mica's challenge two years ago, when she became stranded atop a great stone, surrounded by sandsharks. *Not my fault*, she reasoned.

They all raised a glass and drank to his success. The cool liquid was dark, sweet, and fruity. Amir still looked nervous, but also relieved at having finally come to a decision.

They spent the rest of dinner listening to the story of their father's challenge. Kiva had heard it a hundred times before, but didn't mind it so much this time. The way his face lit up when telling it never failed to make her smile.

Once they finished eating, everyone helped clean up. Kiva did the dishes. She yawned as she placed the last clean plate beneath the counter, then made her way to the cleanroom. She lit a small oil lamp and closed the curtain. Running her hands over the smooth, olive skin of her face, Kiva looked back at her reflection in the polished sheet of metal.

Her hair was so dark brown it might as well have been black. Much of it hugged the sides of her scalp in tight braids. The top of her head was covered in loose, criss-crossing braids that had come undone at the back, falling loose over her shoulders.

She looked into the large, almond shaped eyes staring back from her reflection. Even in the dim light, she could see the bright yellow spikes of color thrusting out from her pupils into the prevailing violet of her irises.

Am I really going to do this? she asked herself silently.

For the past several months, she had been planning something for the proving ceremony. Something no one would see coming. Something that would likely see her ostracized, or perhaps even exiled…and that was if she succeeded. Failure would almost certainly mean death.

When Kiva first came up with the idea, she never actually planned to go through with it. The whole thing was just for fun—Make believe. Something a child would pretend, but never dream of actually doing. But the more Kiva pretended, the more real it became, and before long she found herself preparing in earnest.

She took a deep breath. She *was* sorry she wouldn't be there for Amir's proving.

Kiva stripped off her clothing, kicking it aside and dipping her scrub cloth into the shallow watering pan. Once the sweat, dirt, and grime were washed from her skin, she squeezed water from the soiled cloth over a concave sheet of fabric hanging above. The water dripped as it fell back to the watering pan, filtered by the fabric.

By the time she finished, she was certain. This year would be her year, for better or for worse. With that, she lifted her long white shift from a hook on the wall and pulled it over her head. She scrubbed her teeth with a small wooden brush and rinsed with fresh water; then brushed out the braids from her hair, and left the clean-room. After wishing her parents and brothers goodnight, she retreated to her bedroom. A good night's sleep would be needed to remain at her best the next day. Thankfully, being the only female sibling meant she didn't have to share a room with anyone. *One of the few perks.*

After closing the curtain, she set the lamp down on the floor, beside her bed of softened skins and thinly woven sheets of desert cotton. A gentle breeze blew in through the high circular window, raising goosebumps on her skin. Kiva quickly crawled under the covers.

She was reaching to turn off the small oil lamp when her father's voice spoke from outside the curtain. "Daq Daqun."

"Come in," she said. Her father pushed aside the curtain and stepped inside.

"Daughter, I would speak with you a moment," he said.

Kiva sighed and sat up on her bedding.

Her father stepped forward and lowered himself onto a broad circular pillow. "You know your mother loves you very much," he said.

Kiva looked down at her hands. She could tell where this was going. "I know," she said. "I am sorry I disappeared this afternoon. The weavers hall is just so…"

"Boring?" he finished her sentence, and Kiva looked up at him, smiling.

"I'm no good at weaving," she said, "I don't have the patience for it."

"Patience is a skill one must master, regardless of sect."

Kiva didn't respond.

"Listen, Kivanya, it is as my grandfather used to say, 'Life is like the precious stream of water that flows across the stones in the wet season.'" He gestured with his hands, and Kiva couldn't help but smile. His metaphorical life lessons rarely held much relevance to the situations at hand.

"It travels in all directions," he continued, "flowing continuously until it again joins with the great oceans beneath the stone. Your mother's life flows along the weaver's path. As of now, yours does as well, but that does not mean it must always be so. Our lives often take the same path as those before us, guided by the deep channels worn in the stone by previous generations. But over time, many come to forget that the channels themselves would not exist, had the first few drops of water not dared to flow where none had before."

Kiva nodded. This was actually one of the rare cases where his metaphor made sense.

"If you would like to apprentice for another sect, then you must tell your mother the truth."

Kiva sighed. "If I told her the *truth*, she'd be furious," Kiva muttered. And so would you, she thought.

"Undoubtedly," he said, and Kiva sagged.

He placed a hand on her shoulder and continued, "…at first. But she loves you dearly, Kivanya. Though you may not think it, she desires your happiness above all else. You just need to explain to her that your path lies elsewhere, if that is how you feel."

"If only it were that simple," she sighed, and looked up into his eyes. "Do you promise that you will always love me, no matter the path I choose?"

"Without hesitation, even if you forsook all sects and chose life as an urchin, begging for scraps outside the basin," he said with a grin. "Come, you are only sixteen years in life. You have plenty of time to decide your path and issue a challenge of your own. Now is the time to enjoy your freedom, and support your brother in his own proving."

Kiva felt a stab of guilt. *Am I being selfish?* She pushed the thought away.

"Yes Papa," she said.

"Good," he said, standing. "I will see you in the morning. Tomorrow is a big day! Goodnight, dear one."

"Goodnight Papa…thank you," she said, stifling another yawn.

"You are welcome, little moon." He walked toward the curtain, then paused and turned. "Oh, one more thing."

She looked at him questioningly.

"No more climbing with your brothers. It is *far* too dangerous, and behavior unfit for a young woman."

"Yes papa," she said, averting her eyes.

"Pleasant dreams," he said before slipping out.

Kiva blew out the lamp, lay down, and prayed that her family would forgive her for what she was preparing to do.

THE PROVING CEREMONY

Kiva awoke to the sounds of fast paced, rhythmic drumming and the tinny *clang* of hand cymbals echoing from the basin below. She stretched, then glanced up at the window to find mid-morning sunlight streaming in.

I overslept! She scrambled out of her bedding. By the sound of it, the proving ceremony celebrations had already begun. The smell of fresh roasted meats wafted up, and Kiva could hear laughter, children playing and merchants shouting.

She lifted one of the seating pillows and collected the black tunic and cloth pants from their hiding place. Pulling her shift over her head, she quickly dressed in the surreptitious outfit, before covering it with her normal clothing. She burst from her room, then stopped, running back in to grab a black head wrap, which she tucked inside her white tunic.

Kiva slid into the dining room, which was now empty.

Al'ama! They've already left!

She grabbed a halu fruit from a bowl on the table and rushed out the front door.

Kiva's senses were assailed by the revelry taking place in the massive, curving basin. Her mouth watered at the smell of roasting meat, mingled with the floral scents of alshaysha smoke and incense. There were great baskets filled with seeds, spices, and colorful fruit, as well as stands with scarves in every color imaginable. The varied, hollow beat of drums and high pitched jingle of hand cymbals competed with loud laughter and spirited conversation, as small children danced before the performers. Today was the day of proving, and everyone was celebrating.

Kiva quickly scrambled down the steps toward the basin floor, skirting around those who descended far too slowly, and ignoring their curses. She scanned for her family as she hurried along. Their destination was known to her, but she hoped to find them before they arrived, if for no other reason than to avoid the shame of her late start. Despite her rush, Kiva couldn't help smiling. It seemed everyone was in a good mood. The excitement of the proving challenges was infectious.

"Roasted sahalia! Fresh roasted sahalia!" called a merchant, weaving his way through the crowd holding a bundle of long sticks. Kiva reached in her pocket for a scarab shell, and quickly exchanged it for one of them as she passed. She brought the end of the stick toward her mouth and took a bite of the spiked, roasted lizard.

Kiva hadn't seen her family yet, but would hopefully find them soon. The ceremony commencement stage was atop one of the low, flat stone formations against the eastern wall of the basin. Finishing the sahalia, she hurried through the crowds, still searching. Soon, the raised stone of the ceremony stage came into view. Her father would be the easiest to spot in a crowd, given his size.

After nearly an hour, she still had not found them, and

Kiva began to worry. The commencement ceremony would soon begin, and she hoped to make an appearance before leaving to execute her own plan. That way she could at least show the respect of being present when Amir issued his challenge.

Suddenly the crowds surrounding the stone platform quieted, and Kiva looked up to see Sidi Yehiel—the eldest of the sect of mystics—climb the steps leading to the stage, leaning heavily on a gnarled wooden cane.

Kiva stepped up on the tips of her toes, searching desperately.

There!

She spotted the top of her father's dark green shemagh, wrapped around his head. Kiva quickly weaved her way through the crowd toward him, where she also found her mother, and Mica.

Her father smiled. "Welcome Kivanya. You're just in time," he said.

"I see you finally found your way out of bed," her mother said, raising an eyebrow.

Kiva grinned sheepishly, and before she could respond, the elder mystic began to speak.

His voice was surprisingly strong considering his aged, bent stature, ringing out over the respectfully silent crowd.

"Today, we live and breathe by the will of the great protector, Ahn Ket Suun."

The crowd responded in unison, "We give thanks."

"May The Protector watch over us, and keep us."

There was a pause as the mystic looked out over the crowd.

"This is a sacred day. It is the day many of our young ones will take their first step toward adulthood. It is a tradition going back hundreds of years, to the very settlement of our people in this land."

Kiva mouthed the words along with the mystic. It was the same speech every year, and she'd heard it enough times to know it by heart. She glanced down, and saw a black sleeve peeking out. She quickly tucked it back in. Her mother noticed her fidgeting, and gave her a look. Kiva rolled her eyes, and listened to the same boring lecture she'd heard many times before.

"…let us remember, that this peace came with great cost. For centuries, the Qatal Sharun ravaged our people…"

Kiva stifled a yawn. *More fairy tales,* she thought. After what felt like an eternity, the mystic tapped his cane on the rock three times.

"And now, let those step forward who would issue the challenge."

The crowd turned their eyes toward the stairs leading up to the stone stage, and watched as five boys and four girls ascended, each dressed in elaborately embroidered, ceremonial robes.

"State your name, and tell your people which sect you aspire to join."

Amir was at the front, and the first to step forward.

"I am Amir Masai Fariq, son of Haruk Fariq. I respectfully issue my challenge to the stonemelter sect."

Kiva looked up to see a smile on her parents face, and found herself smiling as well. She and Amir often fought like sand lizards, but that didn't mean she wasn't proud of her *slightly* older brother.

Amir stepped back, and the others came forward one at a time, each issuing their own challenges to the various sects. One girl challenged the weaver sect, another the songmaker sect. The other two challenged the clayform and spicemakers sects. The boys issued challenges to the builders, safekeepers, stormwatchers, and stonegrowers sects.

Kiva could almost feel the crowd's disappointment that there were no challenges to the windwalker or shadestalker sects. These always proved the most exciting, but were the most deadly. It had been years since any were challenged, and their dwindling numbers showed it. Some said the sects would soon dwindle to nothing, given their lack of purpose. Both were formed to protect the Sahra' from ancient enemies. Enemies that none had seen for hundreds of years.

Windwalkers kept watch, flying high over the desert sands to ensure that the Sahra' knew of any and all possible threats well before they arrived. They were also the few who knew the secrets of what lay beyond the desert, in lands forbidden to all else. The shadestalkers were trained for offensive strikes, seeking out and destroying any threats to the people of the basin. Their ways were shrouded in secret, and mothers would often tell tales of the Sharun demons they once fought, to scare misbehaving children.

Despite the lack of challenges to these sects, there was still a certain electricity flowing through the crowd in anticipation of the performances and tests that would soon commence.

After the last young man spoke his challenge, the mystic once again stepped forward.

"With the guidance of The Protector, allow each of these young people to go forth, and face their destiny!"

With that the drums thrummed to life, and the crowd cheered as the small group of youths did their best to appear confident. Once dismissed, they walked off the stage, each heading toward the ceremonial proving ground for their chosen sect.

Amir had spoken first, and so would be the first to face his proving. The stonemelter sect's proving forge was toward the northeastern end of Madina Basin, around the mataqus bend. Amir led the way, and the crowds parted before him. Hundreds of friends, family and strangers followed after him, all eager to witness the demonstration of skill required for entrance into the sect.

It was at this time that Kiva slipped away to enact the plan she had been preparing for.

Trials

Kiva weaved her way through the throngs of people, ducking her head low. Her destination was one that should be relatively calm, compared to this part of the basin. Her theory soon proved true, as the crowds thinned the further north she traveled. She hurried along for several more minutes before finally arriving. Before her stood another low stone platform, butted up against the basin's towering walls. At the back, an entrance had been cut into the wall—a large, peaked archway blocked off by flat stone.

Kiva climbed onto the platform and placed a hand on the craggy wall of stone, stretching ever upward. She tilted her head nearly all the way back, taking in the expansive climb, leading up toward the clear blue sky above. As she did so, she spotted a kiraeen soaring high on the thermals. Its wings and feathered legs were spread wide to catch the warm air, the sunlight reflecting turquoise flashes off its black iridescent feathers.

This was it. The windwalker proving ground. The task itself was fraught with danger. She had spent the past several months learning everything she could about it. The proving was created to test for the three major qualities required of a windwalker. The first was fearlessness of heights. She would need to ascend the stone before her, climbing hundreds of feet up to the cavernous opening above. The second quality was a spiritual connection to the kiraeen. Atop the walls of Madina Basin lay the roosting grounds of the male kiraeen. Some were bonded by their windwalkers, and others still wild. Kiva had always possessed a special talent for communing with the animal life of the desert. She hoped it would be no different with the kiraeen.

From one of them she would need to collect a single feather. The third and final quality to be tested was windfaith. A windwalker must become one with the wind, trusting implicitly in its ability to preserve and protect the kiraeen riders. Kiva envisioned this to be the most challenging and deadly of the tests.

No one had ever attempted a windwalker proving without issuing a formal challenge to the sect, but Kiva knew they would never allow it, if she asked. There would undoubtedly be an uproar at a female attempting the challenge. Should she fail, she would be dead anyway. But should she succeed, she will have proven the tradition wrong. A woman can indeed become a windwalker. With the challenge completed, they would *have* to allow her into the sect.

Kiva nodded, resolute. She quickly hopped down beside the stone platform. After checking to make sure no one was watching, she removed her outer layer of white clothing, revealing the black tunic and pants underneath. She lifted the black shemagh she had tucked away, and wrapped it around her head, hiding everything but her eyes.

Kiva quickly tucked her white clothing behind a stone and leapt back up onto the platform. With a final breath to steady her nerves, she began to climb. The ascent was a challenging one, with few handholds and cracks to make use of. But Kiva had been climbing with her brothers for years. Her experience allowed her to pick out the best path up the sheer stone surface. As she did, the tinny *clink* of the forging hammer rang out through the basin—Amir's proving was underway.

The sun beat down as Kiva clawed, stemmed, and lifted herself toward her goal. After nearly an hour, her fingers and forearms were aching. She scanned for a good spot to rest, and found a wide crack several feet up. She soon reached it and climbed inside. She extended one leg, pressing her foot against one side of the crack, and her back against the other. With her other leg tucked up beneath her, she allowed her arms to dangle at her sides. Kiva rolled her neck, then reached for the small bladder tied to her belt, and took a drink.

The people below were a varied mass of reds, blacks, greens, yellows, and grays, crowding around the proving stage of the stonemelter sect.

Not far above was the halfway point, marked by a small alcove with a bell hanging inside.

Moments later, a cheer erupted from below. There was no mistaking its meaning—Amir's proving was a success. He'd been accepted into the stonemelter sect.

Kiva smiled as she resumed the climb, and after several more minutes, reached the halfway point. The small alcove wasn't large enough for her to climb into, but it did allow her to rest with her forearm flat against its surface. She placed a hand against the large, brass bell, and grinned at the surprise it would elicit.

Kiva shoved, and the bell *clanged* loudly. She glanced down to see tiny, upturned faces within the crowds. Normally, the ringing would be followed by uproarious cheers, but the only sound was that of the bell, echoing off the surrounding stone. Those below began pointing, and soon the crowds started migrating toward the windwalker proving ground.

Satisfied, Kiva continued her ascent. After nearly another hour of the laborious climb, fatigue began to set in. This was more than she had ever attempted with her brothers. Kiva stemmed between a deep crevice, and looked down. Those below weren't much more than colorful dots.

The screech of a nearby kiraeen caught her attention, and she tucked herself deeper into the crevice, hoping it wouldn't notice her. Normally the bonded creatures would not behave aggressively toward challengers, but all before her had been boys. It was said the male kiraeen, bonded or not, were not very accepting of women. *I will give them no choice but to accept me,* she thought defiantly.

Kiva waited a moment, then scanned the sky. There was no sign of the kiraeen, and she resumed her climb. The wind buffeted her back, cooling the sweat on her body. She glanced up, and spotted it—a cavernous opening in the rock face. Kiva had nearly reached the entrance to the kiraeen roosting grounds.

She worked her way up the last several feet, and pulled herself up into the opening.

I made it! she thought triumphantly. Sitting with her legs dangling over the edge, Kiva took another drink, and waved to the crowd below. She could hear the faint sound of half-hearted cheering as the curious onlookers grew in number.

A black shape swooped into her peripheral. Kiva had just enough time to leap back out of the way. A great kiraeen *thumped* down into the tunnel entrance, onto the spot she had been sitting seconds ago. Kiva's heart pounded in her chest. A few paces away, the creature studied her with beady orange eyes, set just above a large, razor sharp onyx beak. Several red feathers, angled back on its forehead, stood starkly against the black feathers covering the rest of its body.

Screeok!

Kiva grimaced, ducking her head at the deafening sound. She looked into its eyes, meeting its gaze directly. Never before had she seen one this close before. The kiraeen was hunched over in the tunnel entrance, forward weight resting on the bent leading edges of its great feathered wings. Black talons extended out from where the wings met the ground.

It's beautiful, Kiva thought with wonder.

"*Sahl,*" she said in a soothing tone, holding up her hand. She held her other hand over the khanjar dagger at her belt.

"*Sahl,*" she said again.

The creature tilted its head, eying her with curiosity. Kiva took a step forward. The kiraeen took up nearly the entire tunnel. If it attacked in here, she might be able to out maneuver it.

The beast must have also been aware of the disadvantage. It leapt backwards out of the tunnel entrance. Kiva ran to the edge of the opening and watched as it spread its great wings, and soared back up into the sky.

Kiva swallowed. There would be many more of them up above, where she would face the second test of her unlawful challenge. She turned, continuing deeper into the tunnel, and came to a set of rough stairs, carved from the rock. She followed the curving staircase, which eventually led to an overhead opening. Bright sunlight streamed through it, illuminating the last few steps. Kiva cautiously ascended, peeking her head out.

The sight she beheld stole the breath from her lungs. She had reached the top of the walls of Madina Basin. The roosting grounds of the windwalker kiraeen. Before her stretched a path with great jutting stone formations, sloping upward on either side. Lodged into the rocks were dozens of kiraeen nests, constructed from sticks, shrubs, bones, and the skins of their prey. Many of the nests were empty, however there were still several occupied with formidable beasts.

Kiva ducked her head back down below, wrestling with the doubt gnawing away at her resolve. Her original plan had been to stay hidden, and steal a feather from one of the nests, but this path put her in direct sight of every kiraeen atop the basin. *How can I possibly keep so many of them away, much less get one of their feathers?*

Kiva imagined facing her family, having attempted the challenge and given up. She pursed her lips in determination. *I've come this far. There is no way I am going back empty handed.* She again poked her head out of the opening and peered down the path. Just then a screech came from above, followed by the rustling of feathers. Kiva followed the sound to where two kiraeen fought in mid-air over the lower half of an agaza lizard carcass. They snapped at each other with large onyx beaks, flapping their wings to stay afloat. Their talons were hooked into the lizard flesh, each refusing to let go.

Kiva watched, captivated by the violent display. One snapped at the wing of the other, tearing out some of its feathers. The injured kiraeen cried out, releasing its grip on the carcass. It flew awkwardly away, perching on a nearby outcropping. The victorious bird let out a screech, and carried the lizard back to a nest high above the rocky path. It tore at the flesh with its razor sharp beak, then lifted its head, allowing the meal to drop down into its gullet.

Kiva watched greedily as the feathers from the injured bird floated lazily down onto the path. "*No!*" she whispered, reaching out helplessly as a sudden gust of wind sent them spinning and whirling.

This is it, she thought. *I need one of those feathers.*

She gathered her courage and bolted up out of the opening, sprinting down the path at full speed. She could hear the screeching cries of the kiraeen, raising the alarm at her presence. She focused on the feathers, which floated down, only to be swept up again, lifted even higher into the sky. Shadows slid across the ground before her as she ran, but her eyes were trained on the lowest feather, dancing its way back down toward the ground.

The wind picked up just as she closed in, but Kiva leapt up onto the sharp, staggered rocks beside the path. She took three quick, climbing strides, and pushed off with all her strength, leaping after the feather. With her arm outstretched, hand open wide, she soared toward it.

Her fingers closed around the iridescent black plume, and she fell back toward the ground. Kiva tucked into a ball as she landed, rolling forward and continuing her run, feather in hand. Her grin was quickly wiped away as a kiraeen swooped toward her. She lunged aside, barely avoiding its large, curving talons.

Still sprinting forward, Kiva squinted, peering ahead. If what she'd learned were true, the third and final challenge should be at the end of the path. Just then, she caught the shadow of another kiraeen swooping toward her from behind. Kiva dove forward, covering her head. She felt a great wind as talons tore into the back of her tunic, narrowly avoiding her flesh.

Once it passed, she scrambled to her feet and bolted down the path. Not fifty paces ahead, the ground sloped suddenly up, ending abruptly. Beyond it would be open air—a great drop all the way back down to the basin floor.

Windfaith, she thought as her legs carried her forward. This was the test she feared most, though with a pack of bloodthirsty kiraeen behind her, she was more than ready to be gone from their roost. The test itself was a leap of faith. A free-fall plunge down a great vertical shaft. There was said to be a consistent wind blowing up through it to slow the fall, but given her pursuers, she would have no time to test it.

Almost there, she thought, pushing her body to its limits.

The kiraeen were relentless, and she was nearly decapitated as another flew by, snapping at her head. Kiva was ten strides from the drop when yet another descended. She managed to avoid its sweeping talons, but one of its wings caught her ankle and she went tumbling.

Rolling and sliding along the hard stone, she eventually

came to a stop, groaning in pain. She pushed herself up, turning to find a powerful kiraeen stalking toward her. Its tail was raised up high, fanned out to display a red pattern of feathers. It weaved the pattern hypnotically in figure-eights. Kiva scooted back frantically, still clutching the feather. The kiraeen crouched low, preparing to strike. There was nothing standing between them, and no time to run. She was caught.

Time slowed, and Kiva watched as the beautiful and deadly creature tensed its leg muscles. The black, iridescent feathers around its head were flayed out, and its orange eyes tracked her with merciless precision. Instinct took over, and Kiva raised a hand up before her. She curled her thumb and the next two fingers into a claw, folding down the last two. She felt her eyes relax out of focus, and she spoke calmly, "Assalamu alaikom, siad Miralaja."

Kiva felt her skin tingle as she reached out to the majestic animal. A primal heat surged through her body, and she felt her mind stretching, expanding toward it.

The kiraeen paused, and she sensed its tension lessen. Slowly, she rose to her feet, keeping her arm outstretched, maintaining eye contact.

"Hudu," she whispered, taking a slow step back. The windfaith trial was several feet behind her. If she could hold its attention long enough...

She took another step, and the kiraeen took a step toward her. It's powerful talons *clacking* against the stone as it did. She took another step, and the creature did the same.

An ember of hope sparked within her; a small distraction from the intense focus she maintained.

She felt a sudden strange recognition within the beast.

Skyhunter, the thought came to her, though it was not her own.

In her peripheral, Kiva caught the dark shape of another kiraeen swooping down. Her eyes instinctively regained focus, and she looked up to see curving black talons speeding toward her. Her connection with the creature vanished, and it screeched in rage.

In a flash, Kiva's dagger was out. She bent her knees, preparing to leap forward. *If I must die, I will die fighting.*

A shadow passed over her, and less than a second later, the diving kiraeen was gone. Kiva looked up and saw several feathers floating down through open air. She quickly turned her attention back to the kiraeen before her. Its eyes were also drawn by events overhead, though it swiftly returned its gaze back to Kiva.

Its tail was once again raised, and its head lowered.

Kiva heard another kiraeen land with a thud behind her.

Here to fight over the meal, she thought. The idea of being torn in two by hungry predators was not one she relished.

Behind her, a deafening screech pierced the air, and Kiva ducked her head. The kiraeen before her was now fixated on whatever had made the noise behind her. It took a step back. Kiva swallowed, and slowly turned around, her heart pounding in her chest.

Raised up on its legs, with great, powerful wings outstretched, was a massive, imposing kiraeen—the same she had seen in the tunnel. Red feathers on top of its head marked it different from the others that had attacked. In her awe, Kiva understood that this was no ordinary creature.

It dove forward toward her, and Kiva dropped flat to the stone, covering her head. The wondrous creature continued past her, crashing into the other kiraeen.

Kiva experienced a brief moment of shock at still being alive, then quickly stood, collecting her wits. Straight ahead was the great drop; the trial of windfaith. There was nothing left standing in her way. Without hesitation, Kiva sprinted forward, clutching her dagger in one hand, and the feather in the other.

Painful animal cries screeched out from behind her as she ran up the sloping path. She reached the end of it at full speed and leapt into the great abyss.

WINDFAITH

Kiva's eyes widened as she soared out over the drop. She was immediately hit with a blast of warm air as she descended, face down, into the dark, seemingly bottomless shaft. The light from the sun above grew dim, and she could no longer discern how quickly she fell.

Kiva closed her eyes, doing her best to eliminate all fear from her mind.

I trust in the wind, she thought, allowing it to bear her downward. As she fell, her sense of time and space became strangely distorted. She no longer felt as if she were falling, but instead experienced a sense of weightlessness.

This must be how they feel, she thought, imagining herself a kiraeen, soaring high above the desert sands. A sense of elation flooded through her as she became one with the wind. She was no longer imagining, but experiencing what she had always longed for. She was the kiraeen, performing an intricate, flowing dance with the wind itself. She felt the power of the wind's caress, and the playful way in which it gusted and eddied. Her body was lifted, turned, released, and caught.

Kivanya found peace, and she decided in that moment that even if it were her last, she would die without regret.

As if in answer to the thought, she was violently yanked

from her experience by a physical shock to her entire body.

Kiva tried to gasp, and her mouth filled with water. She was still floating, only now it felt that all her movement was slowed and restricted. Her entire body stung, but there was no time to think about it. Her lungs screamed for air, and her mind was on the brink of panic.

She pulled off her headscarf, which had slipped down over her eyes, and clawed up toward the wavering pinpoint of light above. After what felt like ages, her face finally breached the surface. Kiva gasped for air, flailing her arms in an attempt to stay afloat. She fought to keep calm, taking a deep breath and holding it. With her cheeks puffed out and lungs filled with air, she found it somewhat easier to keep her head above water.

Kicking her legs, Kiva awkwardly turned herself around in the darkness. Her eyes found a faint shadow that was slightly less dark than everything else, and she floundered toward it.

Her feet soon encountered a rock surface, sloping upward. The water grew more and more shallow, until she was able to crawl up out of it, onto dry stone. She lay there, panting in the dim light cast from a nearby opening.

Kiva's eyes widened suddenly, and she realized her hands were empty. She felt a pang of regret at losing the dagger her father had crafted for her, but the loss of the feather was devastating. Without it she would fail the trials, and all of this would count for nothing.

She rolled over to find the feather floating lazily in the water beside her. Kiva breathed a sigh of relief and snatched it up, slipping it under her belt. Her headscarf hung unraveled, still barely tucked into the neckline of her tunic. She wrung it out, and re-wrapped her head, covering her entire face except for her eyes.

She then walked toward the opening ahead. It was another tunnel, sloping upward. The light grew brighter as she followed it, until she reached the opening, lit by daylight. Beyond it, she could hear the chatter of the hundreds of people who would be waiting to see whether she had survived, and who she was.

She took a deep breath, and realized she had been wrong. The most difficult part of the trial was not windfaith, but facing the windwalker sidi, and her people afterward. Kiva gripped the black kiraeen feather, and stepped bravely out onto the windwalker proving stage. Everything was bright white, as Kiva squinted, waiting for her eyes to adjust. A few in the crowd began to shout and clap. Realizing she had survived, others joined in, and as Kiva's pupils shrank into pinpoints in the bright light, she took in the vast, cheering crowd surrounding the stone platform.

Kiva grinned, and thrust the feather up into the sky. The crowd went berserk. None of them had been anticipating a windwalker challenge, which made it all the more exciting.

Kiva spotted her brother Mica near the front, only he wasn't cheering. He was watching closely with intense curiosity, most likely trying to discern who might be beneath the headscarf.

A moment later, Sidi Jado stepped forward, approaching the crowd with arms outstretched. Kiva hadn't even noticed him standing to her left.

Jado waited patiently for the crowd to quiet, which it eventually did. Even the musicians paused, eagerly waiting to discover the identity of the mystery challenger.

"People of the Sahra," he projected loudly, and the stone walls of the Madina Basin reflected his words back at him. "As you know, there have been *no* formal challenges issued to the windwalker sect."

"He completed the trials!" someone in the crowd shouted.

"I saw him make the climb with my own eyes!" another added.

Kiva could not see his face, but she suspected Jado was displeased by the interruptions. His reputation was one of strength, sternness, formality, and tradition. She had worried he might reject her outright for not having permission to attempt the trials. But she had the crowd on her side…for now.

After a pause, Jado continued, "I am most dissatisfied with the lack of respect in which this *illegal* challenge was issued."

Kiva's shoulders slumped.

Jado looked out over the crowd, and Kiva suspected he was waiting to punish any who might interrupt again. He let the words hang long in the air, before continuing, "*However*…it would seem the spirits do not share my disdain. The unorthodox challenger has survived." The crowd again began cheering exuberantly as he turned back and leveled a hard gaze at her, then once again faced the throngs. "Beyond this, the challenger bears a kiraeen feather…Come forward!" he commanded.

Kiva's heart was racing. It threatened to explode from her

chest. She stepped forward toward the edge of the platform where Sidi Jado stood.

They stood facing each other. Jado's piercing light blue eyes gripped her, as if seeking to probe the very secrets of her soul. Kiva held his gaze. She had stared down a kiraeen as it prepared to disembowel her; she could stare down this man.

Eventually, he spoke, "Who then, so brazenly beseeches the windwalker sect, without so much as a *whisper* of a challenge?"

This was it. The moment that would determine whether she would achieve her dream, or be shunned by her people. Everything boiled down to what happened next. Kiva had imagined it hundreds of times, and even practiced what she might say. It was fortunate she had, for she was under such stress she'd have remained silent otherwise.

Kiva gripped the end of her headscarf, and began to unravel it. As she did, Sidi Jado's eyes grew wide in shock, and his stern look of disapproval was replaced with outrage. She could hear the whispers of the crowd as they realized what she was. Kiva prayed the crowd would judge her by her accomplishment, and not her gender. It was her only hope.

"I, Kivanya Raisel Fariq, have completed the proving, and humbly request to join the windwalker sect." Kiva knelt down bowing her head, and presented the feather to Sidi Jado.

She was motionless, waiting. She had done what she could, the rest was out of her hands. A faint screech came from above, and Kiva felt the wind tugging at the feather she held out before the windwalker sidi.

It was suddenly snatched out of her hands. She looked up

to see Sidi Jado glaring down at her. In his eyes was a whirlwind of indignation and disbelief.

At least I have proven that it can be done, she thought. *I am the first woman to pass the windwalker trials.*

"Stand," he said, still scowling.

Kiva slowly stood, sparing a glance at the crowd. The faces she glimpsed were not nearly as upset as Sidi Jado, however there was no approval in their eyes either. She caught Mica's eye, and his expression was one of fear and worry.

The tension was thick as Kiva again met Sidi Jado's eyes.

"Even if I were to ignore your blatant disregard for the proving ceremony, I cannot ignore the fact that you are a *woman*. You, who would disrespect me, and every windwalker before me, now wishes to join our sect?"

Kivanya swallowed. She had anticipated such a response, but imagining it and experiencing it were two different things entirely.

"You have *no right* to attempt the sacred trials. Your mere presence among the kiraeen is a grave insult to all that we stand for."

"You are *wrong!*" Kiva shouted, before realizing what she was doing. There was a brief moment of shock on Jado's face, and Kiva took advantage of the opening.

"The windwalkers exist to keep watch over our people," Kiva turned partly toward the crowd, addressing them as well. "Is a warning of danger worth less coming from a female? Are fewer lives spared as a result?" Kiva felt her blood rising. It wasn't *fair* that she should be judged as less worthy, simply because she wasn't a man.

"The answer is *no!*" she shouted. "I do not disrespect the windwalker sect, I honor it with every part of my being. I have peered into the soul of the kiraeen, and found my own reflected within."

"Enough! Blasphemous girl!" Jado yelled, finally snapping out of his shock.

Shouts had begun coming from the crowd, though Kiva couldn't tell whether they were in support of her, or Jado.

"I am no *girl*," she said, focusing all of her anger and frustration to a razor's edge. "I am a *skyhunter*."

Jado's surprise returned once again, and was quickly replaced with red-faced rage.

"*Enough!*" he shouted. "You will never be one of us. Your challenge is denied!"

Jado spun on his heel and stormed away, disappearing into the entrance Kiva had come out of moments ago.

She was left alone on the stage, facing the unsettled crowd. Some of them appeared concerned, perhaps they even agreed with her. But others, nearly all of them men, wore looks of anger and disapproval. Something flew up toward her from the crowd, and she ducked. Soon there was more shouting, and Kiva took a step back. She glanced behind her and saw a large stone rolled across the opening behind.

Someone else threw a piece of fruit at her, catching her in the shoulder. Kiva took another step back, as fear rose in her belly. She'd known her plea might be rejected, but had never imagined people would turn on her like this. She looked to find her brother Mica, but he was gone.

More waste was thrown up toward her, and the shouting

grew more intense. Kiva's eyes darted back and forth. She was surrounded, with nowhere to run. An angry man with a full beard covering most of his face climbed up onto the stage. He quickly dashed toward her and grabbed her by the hair.

"No!" she shouted, swinging her fists and trying to shove him away.

Suddenly he released her and collapsed to the ground. Kiva looked and found her brother Mica, standing protectively before her.

"*Quickly!*" he urged, "Come with me."

He placed his arm around her shoulder, shielding her from the refuse, and led her over to the side of the stage. Waiting there were several men, all with the sides of their heads shaved. These were the men of Mica's sect, Kiva realized—shadestalkers.

They formed a protective barrier around her, and led her through the raucous crowd. Even the angriest of those knew better than to tangle with the shadestalkers. The crowd parted like water to allow the deadly escort passage.

"Where are we going?" she asked.

"We are taking you somewhere safe," Mica answered.

The moment was surreal, and Kivanya was beginning to understand that many of her people, if not all of them, had rejected her. She would never again be free to walk amongst them without fear of reprisal.

She and her escort eventually reached an area of the basin that Kiva was unfamiliar with. They slipped inside a discreet opening in the stone wall, and all the shadestalkers save Mica departed. He led her in silence along a passage and up a set of stairs. They continued through an empty common room, down yet another hall, and up several more flights of stairs, until they finally arrived in a long hall with several large, wooden doors. It was rare to see anything other than a curtain at the threshold of a room, and Kiva might have asked about it under different circumstances.

Mica unlocked and opened one of the doors, revealing a simple yet comfortable room with bedding, sitting pillows, a water jug, and a shakh pot. There was a small circular window hole looking out from high above, onto the desert. The floor was covered in a plush decorative rug that Kiva immediately recognized. The pattern was one her mother often used in her own weaving.

"Is this your room?" Kiva asked.

"You will be safe here for the time being. I have to get back out there and try to sort out this mess," he said. "Do *not* leave this room, Kivanya. If you are caught outside it, they will put you in the prisoners' cells below."

He turned to leave, but Kiva grabbed his sleeve. "Mica wait…" she looked at him, fighting back the tears. "Are you angry with me as well?"

Mica sighed, turning to look her in the eyes. "I am not angry at you, Kiva, but I worry what those who *are* might try to do."

"You think I'm foolish, don't you? That I don't deserve to fly?"

"Without question, what you did was foolish."

Kiva slumped, hanging her head.

"But it was also incredibly brave," he continued, "and

more excitement than there has been in the past ten proving ceremonies." Mica smiled. "People will be talking about this for years to come."

"Jado was so angry," she said hopelessly. "I just thought if I could…"

"Jado is always angry," Mica responded, placing a hand on her arm. "Were it up to me, I'd have accepted you then and there."

"Really?" she asked, looking up at him.

"Really. But unfortunately, it's not my choice to make. At this point I just want to make sure no one does anything rash. Just do me a favor and stay put. I'll come back once I know what's happening. Promise me you'll wait here."

"Okay," she said. "I promise."

"Lock the door," he said, before turning to leave.

Kiva stepped inside, and her brother closed the door behind her. She locked it, and walked over to the bedding, collapsing into it. It was as if her body were only now realizing how physically and emotionally exhausted she was. Her eyes drifted closed, and by the time she opened them again, moonlight was streaming in through the high circular window.

A muffled voice came from behind the door, "Kiva, it's me. Open up."

Kiva sat up, rubbing her eyes. She stood and unlocked the door, allowing Mica in.

He carried a tray of fresh fruit, chava bread, and dried aga flesh. Kiva took the tray with thanks, and set it down beside the floor pillows. She collected a cup of water from the jug in the corner, and the two of them sat down.

Kiva was ravenous. She took an over-sized mouthful of bread. "What did you find out?" she asked, her words muffled by the food.

"It's bad," he said, "but not as bad as it could be."

Kiva set down the bread. "Bad? What do you mean?"

Mica's expression was serious, but there was hope in his eyes. "I was hoping things would blow over...that people would dismiss the whole thing as a prank."

"It was *not* a prank!" she said, glaring.

"Listen to me Kiva, you know how I feel, but there are many in the basin who do not share the sentiment. If you wish to avoid their wrath, you must abandon that line of thinking."

"Why should I care what they think? Let them seethe. I completed the trials. I have *proven* that I am worthy!" she argued.

"If you want to remain in Madina Basin, then you will have to take their opinions into account," he said somberly.

"If I want to remain? Do you mean..." Kiva couldn't bring herself to say it.

Mica nodded gravely.

Exile.

It was like a punch to the gut. Her worst nightmare was coming true. No one as young as she had ever been exiled from the basin. How could the very people she hoped to protect renounce her so completely?

She wilted, and Mica's expression softened. "It is not likely to happen," he said. "You are young, and haven't caused any physical harm. There will be a council meeting in ten days. If you play it right, you will get off with a light punishment and nothing more."

Kiva put her face in her hands. There was no stopping the tears now.

Mica put his arms around her and pulled her close. "It will be okay," he said soothingly. "We will show them this was all just a big misunderstanding."

Inside, Kiva was a whirlwind of shame, fear, and anger. Most of all anger.

She shoved Mica away. "No!" she glared at him. "You are acting like it is I that have done something wrong."

"Kiva, you broke the rules—"

"The rules are *wrong!*"

Mica took a deep breath. "That may be, but breaking them is not going to change that."

"And why not?" she argued. "Do you honestly think Jado would have accepted a challenge from me? He would have laughed and sent me to the weavers."

"You could have brought it to the council," he said, though he didn't sound convinced.

"Right, a group of wrinkly old qadims are going to change centuries of tradition because a sixteen-year-old girl asked them to? No," Kiva said, shaking her head. "This was the *only* possible way. I have to show them I am worthy."

"It's over, Kiva. It didn't work. You must let go of this foolish dream. The only way the council will absolve you is if you admit it was a mistake."

"So that's how it is then, is it? You would take their side?"

"I am not taking their side!" he said, throwing up his arms in exasperation. "I am on *your* side. I just want what's best for you, and our family."

"And I suppose you are the right person to *decide* what is best for me? You're just like mother."

"If you can't see that avoiding *exile* is the best thing for you, then yes! You need someone else deciding for you."

"I do not need your help. I will prove to them that they are wrong. If I am exiled…then so be it."

"Selfish girl! Do you not see what your actions do to those around you? Our family is *shamed*. They shout insults at us in the open. Amir's place in the stonemelters is at risk."

Kiva looked away, attempting to hide the shame on her face. "Get out," she muttered.

"It is time to grow up, Kiva, and start thinking about people other than yourself."

"I said *get out!*" she reached for the closest object—the remainder of her bread—and threw it at him.

Mica stood, clenching his jaw tightly, his fists balled up at his sides. After a tense moment, he stormed out, slamming the door.

Kiva collapsed onto the bedding, sobbing. She hated to admit it, but he was right. The whole time she had been thinking of what *she* wanted; of the consequences she might face. She hadn't considered the possibility that her family would pay for the risks she took.

It is not fair! her mind shouted back with indignant rage. The firestorm of emotion battled with her shame as she wrestled with her limited options. Fight for her dream—what was rightfully hers—and ruin her family, or give in. Admit fault. Shame herself to the point where she could never look another in the eyes again.

Kiva had never been one for humility. She saw it as weakness; something others would use for exploitation. She sat up and rested her forehead on the palms of her hands. Her heart ached fiercely, and her stomach filled with anxious butterflies as she realized the path she must take.

There was no choice but to admit fault. Kiva could live with putting her own future in jeopardy, but not her family's. Even so, she would rather die than face her people again, after seeing the hate in their eyes. Following the council trial, no matter the outcome, she would choose a life of exile. The conclusion was a great weight that rested upon her shoulders, but there was some relief in having come to a decision.

After the trial, she would never see her parents, Mica, ever again. A tear rolled down her cheek as she realized that she would even miss Amir's complaints.

What's done is done, she told herself in an effort to remain strong.

She looked down at the tray of fruit and dried meat, and pushed it away.

A sudden light *clack* came from her left, and Kiva looked up to find that the moonlight streaming through her window was completely blocked. She immediately stood, furrowing her brow. Something small dropped in through the round hole in the stone wall, and whatever had been blocking the light was suddenly gone.

I am hundreds of feet up, she thought. *What could have...*

There was something on the floor below the window. Kiva walked over and found a rolled lizard skin, tied with a small cord. She cautiously knelt down and picked it up, turning it over.

OUT AND UP

Kiva poked her head out of the window, and found only the vast, open desert. The rocky walls of Madina Basin stretched vertically above and below, lit by pale moonlight. Kiva untied the cord, and the skin unraveled. A black iridescent feather floated out from it, sailing back and forth as it drifted to the ground.

Kiva bent down and picked it up. A chill ran down her spine. *Who would—*

There was something scratched into the animal skin. Kiva held it up to the moonlight.

out and up

Out and up? Kiva re-read it several times, then looked back toward the window. It was large enough for her to fit through…barely. But *we're on the desert side*, she thought. There was no telling how treacherous or high a climb would be.

She began to climb out, then paused, remembering her decision to be responsible, for the sake of her family. She pulled her head back in, and looked down at the feather in her hand, remembering that feeling of flight she'd experienced during the windfaith trial.

Her eyes switched focus from the feather to the plush rug beneath her feet, the same one that bore her mother's favorite pattern.

No, she thought. *I will not allow my family to suffer because of me.*

With great regret, Kiva tossed the skin out the window, along with the kiraeen feather.

She then walked back to her bedding and sat down on it, crossing her legs. Meditation had never done anything for her in the past, but there wasn't much else to do at the moment. Kiva closed her eyes, resting her hands on her knees, and tried to be at peace with what was to come.

She was just beginning to find a hint of inner calm when a rustling came from the window. Kiva opened one eye to see the animal skin on the rug. She opened the other and saw the feather, once again sailing back and forth on its journey to the floor.

Kiva frowned. *Who do you think you are?* she thought, annoyed at the brazen act.

She stood, intending to throw them back out again, when a knock came at the door.

"Who is it?" she asked after a moment, hiding the skin and feather beneath her bedding.

Three more knocks came at the door.

Kiva remembered the terrifying man climbing the stage and grabbing her hair, and immediately scanned the room for anything she might use as a weapon.

"Kivanya Fariq, you open the door this *instant!*" the unmistakable, muffled voice of her mother came from the other side.

Kiva rushed over and unlocked it, and her mother stepped in, closing the door behind.

Ismaela Fariq looked her daughter over sternly, and Kiva stared at the floor, suddenly conscious of her red eyes and tear stained cheeks. She braced herself for the inevitable barrage that would issue from her mother's mouth.

Then, without another word, her mother did something she never would never have expected. Kivanya felt her mother's arms wrap around her as if she were a small child again, hanging from her apron strings.

Kiva stiffened, unsure how to respond to the unusual show of affection, but her mother only hugged her tighter. She was suddenly hit by the realization that she was not alone. Her mother, at least, had not abandoned her. She collapsed into her arms, hugging back just as fiercely. They finally released, and Kiva felt fresh tears welling in her eyes. She saw the same in her mother's.

"I'm so sorry mama," she said. "I never meant to cause trouble for you and Papa."

Her mother pursed her lips together. "Come, let us sit."

They walked over to the floor pillows and seated themselves across from each other.

"You must think me so foolish," said Kiva.

"At first, yes. I did," her mother answered. "But while everyone else was watching those who were shocked and angry,

I was busy observing those who were not…No woman has ever accomplished what you did today."

Kiva was surprised to find a sense of pride stirring within her.

"The looks on the faces of the young girls in the crowd—those who would soon face their own proving—was not one of outrage, but wide-eyed wonder and hope. Before today, none of them had ever dreamed they could accomplish what you did. They saw themselves in you, Kivanya."

Kiva was unsure how to react. She'd never seen her mother like this before. It was as if something within her, something long forgotten, had awakened.

"But our family's reputation…Amir's proving—"

"We will be fine. The stonemelters are *lucky* to have your father and Amir, and they know it."

"And what about you?" Kiva asked, looking up into her mother's eyes.

"Pah!" she said, flicking her hand dismissively. "On the surface, the weavers share the men's outrage, but within the circles, there is talk of change. I will play the part of a mother shamed, but the truth is, I am *proud* of you, Kivanya. What you did, and even more so Jado's reaction to it, have drawn attention to what many Sahra' women have been feeling for a long while."

"The men have been holding us back," Kiva said.

"No," her mother said sternly. "Adversarial sentiments will lead only to resentment and strife." She breathed a short laugh. "Funny, it would seem your father has rubbed off on me after all these years." She returned her focus to Kiva and said, "We will not claim to be better, but we *will* claim the right to challenge. *This* is the path to change."

Kiva resisted the urge to pinch herself. Her mother, her traditional, strict, controlling mother, was speaking of revolution. She thought back to what her brother had said. "Mica believes I should claim that what I did was a mistake…a joke."

"Of course he does. He is a man," her mother said with a half-smile. "He wants what *he* thinks is best for you. As you know, Lalla Netaniah is on the council of seven. I have spoken with her, and she believes the women of the council will support you in your challenge."

Kiva's heart leapt in excitement, then once again sank. "But there are only three women on the council. They won't be enough to offset the men."

"Which is why it is imperative that all Sahra' women—wives, daughters, sisters—all stand united to demand equal representation on the council."

"You mean…"

"A council of eight. Four men, four women."

Kiva's jaw dropped. The council of seven had been enshrined in tradition since Madina Basin was first settled. It was as solid and unchanging as the towering buttes of the Miralaja.

"You think…I should stand my ground?" she asked hesitantly.

"I think that what you do is your decision, Kivanya. Even with everything that's going on, there is still a chance this may result in exile. You now stand at the center of something far greater than yourself."

Kiva took a deep breath, attempting to come to terms with the responsibility implied in her mother's words. "If you are successful…If *we* are successful," Kiva corrected, "and there are four men and four women on the council, what will happen if there is a tie?"

"A good question. Either there will have to be a compromise, or a deciding vote from another."

"Who?"

"Some have suggested the eldest of the sect of mystics."

"But the eldest is also a man," Kiva said, recalling the gnarled old figure who spoke at the proving ceremony commencement.

Her mother nodded. "Yehiel is the eldest, but it will not always be so. His sister, Suriel is the next in line. She would succeed him in the position once he passes."

Kiva nodded. Yehiel deciding would not necessarily help her situation, but the change would be a massive victory for future generations of Sahra' women. "A male tie-breaker *will* make the councilmen more agreeable," she acknowledged.

Her mother smiled with pride. "Precisely."

Kiva gazed at the window, up toward the sky, then turned back to face her mother. She had rejected the idea of fighting for her own selfish reasons, but this was no longer just about her.

"Alright," she said. "I will stand my ground," she said firmly. "Even if it means exile."

Her mother's smile faded, and was replaced with serious determination. She reached out and took Kiva's hand. "I will do everything in my power to prevent that from happening.

You have my support, and that of the weavers."

Kiva once again felt tears fighting to reach her eyes. "Thank you."

"Thank you, for reminding me that there are more important things in life than propriety and *tradition*."

Her mother reached into the bag slung over her shoulder and pulled out a folded black headscarf. "This is for you."

She handed it to Kiva, who took it gently. A red symbol had been embroidered onto its surface. Kiva traced it with her fingertip. It was a kiraeen, all four of its wings spread wide, surrounded by a circle.

"I…thank you." She was too moved to say more.

"Before long, every woman in Madina Basin will be wearing that symbol."

"Mama…I don't know what to say," she looked into her mother's turquoise eyes, and found a new light there.

"You needn't say a thing," she answered.

Kiva leapt into her arms. "Thank you," she whispered.

"You have my love, child, and that of your father. You are not alone."

After a long moment, they released each other, and stood.

"I will try to come back and give you an update," her mother said. "But getting in here was not easy, and might not happen again before you stand before the council."

Kiva realized suddenly, that this could be the last time she saw her mother. "Can you not stay a while longer?" she asked.

Her mother smiled fondly. "Would that I could, but there is work to be done, and only ten days to do it."

Kiva nodded, doing her best to mask her disappointment. "I understand."

Her mother smiled, placing a hand to her cheek. "Stay strong, Skyhunter."

With that, she turned and walked out of the room.

Kiva immediately hurried over to the bedding. She lifted the covers, revealing the lizard skin and kiraeen feather. She held the feather up to the moonlight, watching as turquoise, green and blue colors danced across it. She looked again at the lizard skin in her hand.

out and up

She tucked it into her shirt, and the feather under her belt, before pulling herself up through the window. Above, the craggy face of the basin's outer wall loomed. Kiva chose a path, and began to climb.

JONAH

Kiva ascended, hand over hand, until she reached the broad, flat top of the basin walls. She cautiously pulled herself up onto it, and looked around. It was a clear night. The three quarter moon was shining bright enough to hide most of the stars. Far overhead, a thin, curving band of white stretched from one horizon to the other; though it, too, was dimmed by the moon's splendor.

The top surface of the towering stone walls was flatter here, when compared with the jagged, toothy crags of the kiraeen roost. Kiva walked forward onto the sandy surface, until she stood at the center of a large, circular clearing. She stopped and turned in a circle, observing the weather-worn, natural stone formations surrounding her. Even in the moonlight, she could discern the striated layers of red, brown, and white. Some were pocked with holes high above, and others held darkened caves.

The hairs on the back of her neck stood on end, and Kiva got the sensation she was being watched.

"Hello?" she called out, slowly turning.

There was a scrabble of stone, and the *whoosh* of wind. Kiva spun, and a kiraeen landed, even before she had fully faced it. It lowered its head, which was wreathed in black feathers. Its wings were slightly drawn from its chest, and its tail was fanned out, weaving in hypnotic figure-eights. Kiva knew better than to watch the tail, but she was unarmed.

"Zakai! Ainhasar!" a man's voice came from behind her.

The kiraeen lowered its tail and raised its head, barked a screech of annoyance, and leapt forward into the air. Kiva ducked to avoid being knocked over as it sailed past her and drifted up on the breeze.

She turned to watch it go, and saw the owner of the mysterious voice approaching from behind a stone. Kiva's eyes widened. The young man walking toward her wore the light leather windwalker vest over a black tunic. His dark brown hair, which was neither very short, nor very long, hung in disheveled locks across his forehead. As he grew closer, Kiva saw he was only slightly taller than she was. His eyes locked onto hers. They were mostly green, but like hers, were spiked with yellow.

He stood before her, arms crossed, and raised an eyebrow. "Took you long enough."

Kiva's shock at his rudeness lasted less than a second. "Who do you think you are? Throwing your trash into my window?" she demanded, pulling out the rolled lizard skin and shaking it at him.

"You lost your feather earlier today, I figured you might want it back," he said, a hint of a smile playing on his face.

Her hand went to the feather at her waist. "Sidi Jado rejected my right to challenge."

"Oh I know," he said. "I saw the whole thing."

"Then you should know that I no longer have need of it."

"That so?" he said, glancing at the feather, still tucked into her belt. "Then why not toss it aside?"

Kiva narrowed her eyes. "Who are you? Why have you asked me here?" Her attention was drawn away briefly as the kiraeen landed atop a stone formation behind him.

"I am Jonah Basara, and back there,"—he glanced back, pointing a thumb toward the kiraeen—"is Zakai."

"*We met,*" Kiva muttered.

"Yeah…sorry about that. I had to see if it was really true."

"What?"

"That the kiraeen are compelled to attack women on sight. It would seem they are!" he said, satisfied with the test. "At least the male ones are."

"You said you saw the whole thing…you should already *know* they are aggressive toward me."

"True," he shrugged. "but you were in their roost, stomping around, making a racket. Kiraeen are very territorial, you know…not to mention that female kiraeen showing up."

"I could have been kill—" Kiva furrowed her brow. "The what?"

"The female kiraeen. I am sure you saw her—larger than the others, red feathers atop her head?"

Kiva thought back to her windwalker challenge. The creature that landed in the cavern after her climb, it had red feathers on its head…as did the kiraeen that landed behind her before the windfaith trial.

"Caused quite the stir, that one." A brief look of concern came and went from his face like a passing cloud.

"I don't understand," said Kiva. "I thought the females couldn't be bonded."

"They can't," he confirmed. "Far too aggressive. I've never seen one come this close to the roost before. You know the last man who tried to bond a female kiraeen was eviscerated?" Jonah made a hook with his finger and dragged it across his belly.

Kiva gave him a look of disgust. "Have some respect. He was a windwalker, like you."

Jonah shrugged. "It was a hundred years ago. I'm sure he's over it." He grinned.

Kiva rolled her eyes, doing her best to ignore his undeniable charm.

"I saw the female circling in the morning," he continued, "and decided to follow her…make sure she didn't kill any bonded kiraeen. That's when I spotted you. Turns out she and I were both curious. She too took an interest in your windwalker challenge."

"So you saw the kiraeen hunting me, and did nothing?"

"Oh I did plenty," he assured. "I kept Zakai from joining in the frenzy when you stirred up the roost. Had I not been on his back, he'd have been on yours in seconds. Zakai is faster than any of his brothers."

Kiva didn't answer, but she noted with respect how he spoke of his kiraeen with such pride.

"Besides," he said, "you didn't need my help. That female kiraeen did more than I ever could have."

Kiva shook her head. "She tried to kill me, just like the others."

"She *saved* you. More than once. Only a female could have challenged so many…they are incredible creatures."

Saved me... Kiva had been so focused on her survival she'd missed what was in plain sight. The kiraeen had been protecting her from the males. That was why she hadn't attacked in the tunnel.

"You still haven't answered my question," she said, focusing on the present. "Why have you asked me here?"

Jonah met her gaze, and the humor slipped from his face. "What you did, challenging in secret, was either very brave, or very stupid."

Kiva frowned, placing her hands on her hips.

"But it was also an extraordinary display of talent. The effortless climb, the way you faced down that kiraeen…and the windfaith—zero hesitation. Spectacular!"

As if I had any choice, she thought. Kiva relaxed slightly, but refused to give any indication of how much the compliment meant to her.

"Jado is old fashioned," said Jonah. "He thinks that if we simply hold to the old ways, things will go back to how they were."

"What do you mean, how they were?"

"Windwalker numbers have dwindled over the years. People have begun to forget how vital we are to the survival of the Sahra', simply because there haven't been any large-scale attacks in the past two-hundred years. But the signs are there. This peace will not last forever. We must change… adapt." He pounded a fist into his open hand, gazing off over her shoulder.

"Signs? What signs?" Kiva asked.

"Hm?" his attention returned to her. "Oh. One thing at a

time. We need more windwalkers, and thanks to you, I think I know how to make that happen."

"Thanks to me?" Kiva asked.

Jonah again turned his eyes to hers. He was so sure, so confident. Kiva couldn't help being drawn in by his raw determination.

"I'd like to train you to bond with your own kiraeen, and become a windwalker."

Kiva's jaw dropped. "You want to train me…"

"Yes."

"To be a windwalker?"

"What do you say?" he asked.

"But Sidi Jado—"

"What Jado doesn't know won't hurt him."

"But if he ever found out…you could be expelled from the sect."

Jonah laughed. "My Uncle denies the very existence of anything he doesn't want to believe. He won't find out."

"Wait a minute…Jado is your *Uncle?*"

Jonah nodded nonchalantly. "He adopted me years ago…or rather, circumstance landed me in his care."

Kiva frowned. Given everything else going on with the council…this could make things complicated. Kiva studied Jonah's expression, and found herself drawn to him. *Very complicated.*

"I know what you're thinking," he said. "With the trial in ten days, there's no way we'd have enough time—"

"You know about that?" Kiva asked in surprise.

Jonah nodded. "Me, and everyone else in the basin," he

said with a grin. "Your name is on everyone's lips, for better or for worse."

Kiva sighed, pressing her palm to her forehead.

"Listen," he said, placing his hands on her shoulders.

Her skin tingled as if tiny lightning bolts were jumping between them.

"You've got the talent. I know you do. And *I* know windwalking inside out. I grew up on this stuff! We get you on the back of a kiraeen before the trial, and the council will *have* to acknowledge what you are."

"And what's that?" she asked.

"The *first* female windwalker," he answered. "If we can convince them it can be done, they will *have* to open up the sect to men *and* women. Which would mean…" He raised an eyebrow, gesturing for her to finish.

"More windwalkers," she answered.

"Precisely! What do you say?"

Kiva placed a hand on her chin, considering. The fact that Jado was one of the council members complicated things greatly. If it were discovered that his own nephew, adopted or not, was training her in secret, it could derail *everything* her mother and the weavers were working toward. On the other hand, if she were to succeed, it would only serve to strengthen the argument that women deserved equal representation on the council. Then there was Jonah. Somehow she knew he would be trouble, yet the idea of bonding her own kiraeen…

She sighed. *When did everything become so complicated?*

After a long moment, Kiva answered, "Alright. I'll do it."

"Yes!" he shouted.

"On one condition."

"Name it."

"No one can know. Not a soul. Jado *can't* find out."

"Done. My lips are sealed."

"I mean it," she insisted. "There is something going on here that's bigger than either of us. If he finds out, it could mess everything up."

"I got it, no one will know but you, me, and Zakai. He's got a big mouth, but don't worry, no one listens to him anyway."

Zakai chirped a screechy objection from his perch.

Kiva frowned. "This isn't a joke."

"You're right, I'm sorry." Jonah stood straight and placed a hand over his heart. "You have my word, Kivanya Fariq. I will speak not one word of your training."

"Okay," Kiva said, nodding. "I accept your offer."

"Excellent! We begin tomorrow night. Meet me here, one hour after sundown."

Kiva felt a smile spreading across her lips, and fought to conceal it.

I'm going to become a windwalker! she thought excitedly.

"Oh, and don't eat anything beforehand," he added. Jonah put his fingers to his mouth and whistled loudly. Zakai pushed off from his perch and climbed high into the sky, then dove suddenly, falling like a stone.

"Don't be late!" Jonah called, sprinting past her toward the drop.

Kiva watched in surprise as he leapt from the edge of the wall she'd climbed moments ago. Seconds later, he and Zakai rose up again into the night sky.

Show-off, she thought, and grinned despite herself.

Rüh

Kiva spent the following day pacing her room, nibbling on the modest meals brought by shadestalker sect keepers. By late afternoon she'd begun to feel thoroughly stir crazy. There had been no visitors, and Mica's room was decidedly bare, with no games, puzzles, or even any boring scripts to read.

She approached the window and considered climbing out early, then decided against it. If she *did* have a visitor, or if one of the keepers were to return and find her missing…

Kiva sighed, studying the pattern in the rug beneath her feet. She sat down cross-legged and waited, until the sun finally set behind the mountains to the west. *About time,* she thought.

A gentle knock came at the door. "Dinner," a muffled voice called from behind it.

Kiva stood and stretched, then unlocked and opened the door. Behind it was the same keeper who'd brought her meal earlier—an elderly woman in loose fitting gray robes, tied at the waist.

"Thank you." Kiva accepted the tray of food. "No need to come back for the tray," she added, shutting the door. Remembering Jonah's warning, she set it down on the floor, and went to the window. The few clouds in the sky were lit by an array of vibrant pinks and yellows from the dying light beyond the horizon.

One hour.

Soon the light faded, revealing the moon, once again shining brightly down upon the desert.

Close enough, she thought, and pulled herself out into the cool desert air. She began the climb, and soon stood once again atop the walls of Madina Basin. There was no sign of Jonah, so she decided to do a little exploring.

Kiva walked to one of the weathered stone formations and ran her hand along the smooth surface. She continued around it until she discovered a cave, and peeked inside.

"Having fun?"

Kiva nearly jumped out of her skin. She spun to find Jonah, trying to hide an obvious grin with his hand.

She resisted the urge to strike him. "Do you always sneak up on people like that?"

"Unfortunately, no. Most windwalkers can sense the currents well enough to avoid being surprised."

"Sense the currents? How? What do you mean?" she asked, her curiosity winning out over her annoyance.

"Come," Jonah said, gesturing. "Let's begin your first lesson." He turned and walked back to the center of the clearing, and she noticed a cloth bag slung over his shoulder, along with a large canister made from hardened animal skin.

Once there, Jonah reached into the satchel and pulled out a brown leather harness, all straps and iron rings. He held it out, and Kiva took it, turning it over in her hands. The rings had been sewn into it in several places.

"Go ahead," he said. "Try it on."

Kiva held up the harness, eying it skeptically.

"Trust me," Jonah said. "You're going to want to wear that."

Kiva held it before her, and stepped through the loops. She pulled it up, and put her arms through the straps. Jonah stepped behind her, adjusting the straps as she looped the leather through a buckle at the front.

He stepped back, rubbing the stubble on his chin. After one more quick adjustment to her shoulder strap, he nodded.

Kiva adjusted the strap around her thigh. "What is this—"

Jonah interrupted her question with two rapid whistles. Seconds later, they were sharing the clearing with Zakai. Kiva took a step back from him, and his feathers bristled in a wave over his body.

"Now now, you two are going to have to get along if this is going to work."

Zakai chirped, snapping his beak in Jonah's direction.

"Oh quit complaining, you big baby. Kiva's not going to hurt you."

Kiva was on her guard, ready to dive out of the way should the unruly raptor attack. "Me? Hurt *him?*" she asked, incredulous.

"Kiva, try to maintain a sense of calm. Kiraeen are highly attuned to those around them. If you are on your guard, then Zakai will be too. Try to relax."

Kiva took a deep breath, and attempted to calm her nerves. It wasn't easy. One swipe of his talon, and Zakai could open her up like a ripe melon.

"Good," Jonah said, taking a step back.

"Now Kiva, I want you to reach out—"

Kiva stretched her arm out toward the kiraeen.

"No!" Jonah called out as Zakai snapped at her, and she jerked her hand away just in time.

"Let me finish!" Jonah admonished. "Look into his eyes, and reach out with your *mind*."

Right, Kiva thought, willing her hands to stop shaking. *My mind.*

She met the kiraeen's beady orange eyes, and saw his pupils dilate. Her own eyes instinctively relaxed their focus, and she began to feel a tenuous connection forming between herself and the kiraeen. Zakai appeared to calm down, raising his head with his onyx beak slightly agape.

"Good," Jonah said, though his voice sounded strangely far away. "Maintain the connection."

As Kiva drifted through the ether of Zakai's consciousness, she sensed a deep, primal pulsing. Curious as to the source, she followed it, winding her way through the tendrils of animal instinct, many of which were pulled taut as bowstrings. Careful to avoid them, she continued exploring with her mind, until she came upon it. A great, glowing mass of red energy from which everything else emanated.

Zakai emitted a low, gentle cooing sound.

"What are you doing?" Jonah asked. There was concern in his voice, but Kiva was too absorbed to pay much attention.

She continued toward the powerful energy, reaching out for it.

"Stop!" Jonah shouted, but Kiva was so close, and it was

so beautiful. Such raw, unbridled power. It roared like a torrent in her ears as she drew near.

A solid wall slammed into place between them, and the connection was instantly broken. Zakai shook his head, then nearly every feather on his body flared out. He extended his neck, parted his beak and released a deafening screech, inches from Kiva's face. Kiva fell backwards, and Zakai leapt into the air, flying off.

Kiva was shaking, sitting on the ground when Jonah came over. "What do you think you're—"

She looked up at him, wide-eyed and shaking. The anger melted from his face, and he extended a hand to help her up. Kiva took it and he pulled her to her feet.

He asked in a gentler tone, "Are you alright?"

"Huh?" She blinked. "I…I'm fine." The truth was, her head ached fiercely.

Jonah placed a thumb under her eye and moved in to get a closer look. He moved to the other eye, and Kiva suddenly realized how close they were. He was touching her cheek, and his face was inches from her own. She shoved his hand away and stepped back.

"I'm fine," she said, hoping he wouldn't notice the color in her cheeks.

"Who taught you to do that?"

"Do what? I just did what you told me to," she answered.

"Oh I assure you," he said, raising his eyebrows. "You did so much more…Anyone ever tell you it's bad manners to bond another man's kiraeen?" He wore that same small smile at the corner of his mouth again, and Kiva found herself bereft of a response.

"So you nearly bonded a kiraeen with zero training? And here I thought nine days would be tough. You did it the first night!"

Kiva swallowed. She couldn't shake the blast of rage Zakai had directed at her. To Kiva, it didn't at all feel like success. "Zakai…"

"Zakai's *fine*. You just gave him a scare, that's all. Kiraeen are incredibly private creatures. What you saw was his essence…his rüh. You and I are the only ones to have ever seen it."

Kiva felt a wave of shame. She had been witnessing the very soul of this creature, and her first instinct was to reach out toward it like some kind of…*lecher*.

"I…I'm sorry," she said.

"No," he shook his head. "It's my fault. I should have suspected as much. It would seem you have many extraordinary qualities, Kivanya."

Normally Kiva would have corrected him, insisting he call her Kiva, but there was something about the way he said it that didn't bother her so much.

"Let's try again, only this time—"

"Again? You're kidding right? Zakai wants to murder me!"

"Zakai! Tati!"

The kiraeen sprung up from behind one of the stone formations, flapped his great, black wings, and drifted over.

"He's just pouting," Jonah grinned mischievously.

Zakai swooped in close and landed beside him. The wind from his wings briefly rustled their hair and clothing.

"Go on, say you're sorry," Jonah said, giving Zakai a nudge.

Zakai chirped an objection back at him.

Jonah put his hands on his hips and raised an eyebrow.

Zakai turned his head toward Kiva, watching warily.

Strangely, Kiva had never seen him this at ease in her presence before. His wings hung down, bent at the joint, and his long forward talons were lowered.

He took a step toward her. Kiva glanced nervously at Jonah, who nodded encouragement. Zakai slowly extended his long neck, closing his eyes. His beak was inches from her chest.

She once again looked to Jonah, who mouthed, "Go ahead."

Kiva slowly lifted her hand and placed it on his great beak. It was hard, but she hadn't expected it to be so warm. Zakai pushed his head forward, turning it sideways so that her hand rested on the soft down feathers under his beak.

A great smile bloomed on Kiva's face as she realized what he was doing. She gently scratched the feathers as Zakai tilted his head for her. By the time he moved back, she was beaming. Zakai fluttered his feathers, giving a shake that began at his head and ended at the top of his tail.

"There!" Jonah exclaimed. "We're all friends."

"I don't understand," Kiva said, turning to him. "He's not attacking. What changed?"

Jonah pursed his lips and knitted his brow in thought. "When you see a kiraeen's rüh, they see your own as well. It is not possible to bond one against his will—they must see in you a kindred spirit. Perhaps in you, Zakai saw he had nothing to fear."

Zakai chirped.

"Now, we can begin your lesson," Jonah said with a nod.

"Begin? You mean that wasn't it?" Kiva asked.

"*That* was for you and Zakai to become acquainted. How else am I supposed to teach you to fly? Unless you're hiding some feathers back there somewhere?"

"Fly…" Kiva's mouth had suddenly gone dry. "Aren't there some things you'd like to teach me first? What if I fall off?"

Jonah placed his hand onto a strap peeking out from under Zakai's feathers. He lifted a metal clip attached to a ring, and pointed to Kiva.

"Right…the harness," Kiva had forgotten she'd even been wearing it. Butterflies were leaping and bounding in her stomach, and she grasped for an excuse to delay. "But Zakai and I barely know each other…he might not be comfortable enough to fly with me."

"Zakai?" Jonah asked.

Zakai jumped playfully, landing with a *thump.*

"I think he's ready."

Kiva was frozen in place. *Really?* she berated herself. *After everything you've done? You're finally given the chance to fly, and you freeze?*

"Don't worry," he reassured her. "I was nervous my first time too. There's really nothing to it…at least not with Zakai in control." He placed a hand on her shoulder, and she thawed. She allowed him to lead her over to Zakai, who crouched down, lowering himself and extending the wing closest to her.

Jonah guided her to where the leading edge of the kiraeen's

wing met his body. With the wing extended, she could more easily access the harness underneath. Kiva gripped the upper strap with both hands, stepped onto the lower one, and pulled herself onto his back. Once she was seated, he retracted his wing, still crouching. Jonah clipped her harness to Zakai's at the thigh, and instructed her to lean forward. Kiva lowered herself forward, until her forearms were resting on the straps running the length of Zakai's body. Jonah then clipped the rings at the front of Kiva's shoulders to Zakai's harness, and double checked the straps.

Once he was finished, Zakai stood to his normal height. Kiva could instantly feel the strength, a deep well of potential energy within the muscled limbs of the kiraeen.

"If you are going to be a windwalker, you will need to learn what it feels like to soar on the back of a kiraeen. I want you to pay special attention to how Zakai moves. You must learn to trust him, and in turn he will trust you."

Kiva gripped the harness with sweaty hands, and gave a quick nod.

"Trust your instincts," he said. "You're good at that."

Jonah then turned to the kiraeen and called out, "Zakai, *yatir!*"

Kiva's stomach dropped as the great winged raptor leapt high into the air.

First Flight

Zakai beat his powerful wings, and Kiva gripped tight as they were launched forward toward the drop. In the blink of an eye, the ground was gone–replaced with a vast expanse of open air.

Kiva lifted her head, and a blast of wind made her eyes water. She quickly ducked it down once again. Far below, the dimly lit landscape rushed by. Zakai swept his wings back and Kiva clung tightly as they sped forward at even greater speed. Without warning, he shifted his hind feathers and their forward motion was translated into vertical lift. The speed of their climb slowed as gravity exerted its will upon them, and Zakai began to gently loop backward in an arc. Kiva looked up and found the ground far below. A smile of pure joy dawned on her face. This was better by far than anything she'd imagined. Her muscles began to relax.

They reached the apex of the loop and curved back down again, falling with a sensation of weightlessness. Zakai tucked his wings and they gained speed, diving nose first toward the ground. Kiva felt a tensing of Zakai's left hindquarter, and they were suddenly spinning like a top as they fell. She ducked her head against his soft feathers, warding off the wave of nausea assailing her stomach. It was clear now why Jonah had instructed her to skip dinner.

Zakai spread his wings wide, and they swooped back up into the clear, star-strewn sky. They climbed gently on the currents, and Kiva felt a shiver run through her body. *I can see everything,* she thought with wonder. Far off to the east, beyond the desert, the moonlight reflected off a great, looming sea of darkness. She had of course heard of the great ocean to the east, but hearing and seeing were two very different things. Directly below, the desert buttes and mesas were like shadowy pebbles. Zakai slowly turned in a great arc, and Madina Basin came into view. From high above, Kiva could see clearly the tops of the towering walls, and the hollowed out basin within. It was filled with thousands of lights—from the homes of families eating dinner, spending time together. Kiva imagined sharing the experience of her first flight with her own family, and felt a pang of sadness.

As they drifted high over the basin, Kiva thought she could see the light of her old home, and she leaned forward to get a better look. Zakai responded instantly, rolling over into a dive in that direction.

"No!" she cried. If they were spotted flying low over the basin, it would be disastrous. Zakai swept his great wings, hastening the dive. *No no no!* Kiva pressed herself tight against Zakai's body. Her forearms were pushing down into the harness at his sides, and she gripped the straps with white knuckles. *Relax,* she told herself. *Trust your instincts.*

She relaxed the tension in her forearms and hands. Zakai ceased propelling them downward, but they were still free-falling toward the basin. Kiva wracked her brain for a way to control him.

"Ainhasar!" she shouted, but it had no effect.

An idea struck her, and she pulled back on the straps she had been gripping so tightly. Zakai's wings shot out, fully extending. Kiva's stomach did another somersault as they swung back up into the sky, climbing vertically. She pressed gently forward, and Zakai adjusted his rear limbs, causing them to level out. Kiva breathed a sigh of relief as they passed beyond the far walls of Madina Basin, floating gently on the air currents.

Zakai was responding to her cues! *If pushing forward is dive, and pulling back is climb, then what's faster?* Kiva thought back to what Jonah had said when they first took off.

"Zakai, *yatir!*"

The kiraeen instantly thrust his wings back, propelling the two of them into a swift, steep climb. They rose higher and higher, until Kiva felt as if she could reach out and touch the moon. The cool air raised goosebumps on her skin, and she pushed gently forward on the harness straps, until she and Zakai leveled out.

The westward view was stunning. She could see all the way to the edge of the desert, where the arid landscape transitioned into dark, textured forest. It eventually climbed up the base of the great mountain range running north to south.

The sensation of freedom coursing through Kiva was pure bliss. She lay flat on Zakai, closed her eyes, and slowly released her grip on the harness. With her arms extended, she made her hands into flat surfaces that sailed over the wind-stream. Relaxing her thighs, she slowly extended her legs out as well. With her arms and legs extended, Kiva slowly began generating her own lift. The rings of the harness jingled, and the latches became taut as she lifted off Zakai's back. The feeling was indescribable. She was in a perfect balance between the desert and the sky. In complete harmony with all things above, and below. She was bathed in the wind, and it bore her as surely as solid ground.

Kiva opened her eyes, and slowly brought her limbs back in, resting them into their places on Zakai's harness.

"Let's see what you can do!" she said, brimming with excitement.

Kiva pulled back on the harness straps and Zakai looped over backwards into a dive. She yelled out with joy as they plummeted, speeding toward the ground. Kiva pulled again, simultaneously applying pressure with her right foot. Zakai spread his wings, curving back up into the sky, spinning as they climbed together. Kiva released the pressure of her foot, ending their spin, and leaned hard to the right. Zakai peeled off, diving in the same direction.

She tried pulling on just one side, and Zakai extended the opposite wing, causing them to bank sideways, rolling completely over. She pulled on the other and rolled in the other direction, then pulled both and Zakai again swooped up into a climb.

As Kiva soared through the sky on Zakai's back, she was carried away from her worries, her fears, and the pressure to succeed. Up here, she was free from everything. Nothing could reach her. Even exile would be bearable upon the back of a kiraeen.

She continued experimenting, and began taking the wind into account as she gave subtle cues to Zakai. After what felt like a matter of minutes, the kiraeen turned and sped back toward the walls of Madina Basin. Kiva could sense that he traveled with purpose, and made no attempt to divert him. Soon the smooth stone formations atop the basin's wall took shape in the moonlight. A moment later, Kiva spotted Jonah's small figure leaning up against one of them. They drifted toward the same circular clearing they'd taken off from, and with several powerful flaps of his wings, Zakai slowed their speed and landed gently on the stone surface.

By the time Jonah arrived, Kiva had unclipped the two rings of her harness, and was sitting up.

"That was…" Kiva trailed off. She couldn't think of a word powerful enough to describe it, nor could she wipe the grin from her face.

"I know," he said smiling back at her. "The best part? It's like that *every* time…in fact, it gets *better*."

Zakai lowered himself, and Kiva unhooked the latches on either thigh, and slid over his side.

"You two were gone a long time. It's been over an hour," he said.

"An hour? It felt like minutes," she said in all honesty.

"Either Zakai really likes you, or you're a natural."

"Or both," she said with a smile.

Zakai chirped in agreement, and sprung into the air, lifting off to find a comfortable perch.

They both watched him go, then turned to face each other.

"Did you get a good feel for the harness?" Jonah asked. "How he moves?"

"You might say that," she answered with a small smile. The truth was, by the end, she was able to direct him as effortlessly as she would her own limbs.

"Don't get too spoiled," Jonah warned. "No other kiraeen is as responsive as Zakai."

"He is magnificent," Kiva agreed.

Jonah looked her over. "That's all for tonight," he said.

"That's all?" she asked, disappointed. "We just started."

"Hold your hand out flat," he instructed.

Kiva did as he asked. Her hand wavered like a leaf. Try as she might, she could not keep it steady.

"You may not realize it, but flying on a kiraeen can be exhausting. The physical toll, and the concentration required…Go home. Get something to eat, and meet me here tomorrow."

Kiva sighed. He was probably right. She was beginning to feel hunger pangs. "What's tomorrow?"

"Combat training," he answered flatly.

Kiva grinned. With two older brothers—one of whom was now a shadestalker—she'd had plenty of chances to hone her fighting skills. The thought of testing them against Jonah sent a thrill through her, which she quickly suppressed. "See you then," she answered seriously.

Kiva turned, walked to the edge of the wall, and began her descent back to the window of her room. Once in the safety of the sect living space, she lit the oil lamp on the wall and knelt beside the dinner tray she'd left behind. She ate voraciously. Given her appetite, the food tasted incredible.

Full and satisfied, Kiva blew out the lamp, undressed, and lay down in her bedding. Less than an hour ago, she had been hundreds of feet in the sky, diving and swooping. Considering her excitement, sleep came faster than she'd have expected.

THUNK.

Kiva bolted up from her deep slumber, grasping for the dagger she no longer possessed. There was enough moonlight to see she was alone in the room, but her eyes were trained on the door. Slowly, she stood, cleared off the metal dinner tray, and held it in both hands.

She crept forward toward the door and listened.

It was completely silent, save for her breath.

Kiva frowned. That someone would have the nerve to harass her *here,* in the middle of the night! She summoned her anger, banishing the fear that threatened to take over. She unlocked the door, and bracing it with her shoulder, gently opened it a crack to peek out.

No one.

She opened the door a bit wider and looked up and down the halls. They were completely empty, but there was something on her door. A ten inch steel spike had been driven into it, holding up a dried, flat lizard skin. Scratched into the skin was a single word:

OUTCAST

A shiver ran through Kiva's body. She was unused to having enemies, and this place was home to the Sahra's most lethal sect of assassins. The chances of someone breaking in from the outside were slim. She swallowed, and took one more look before yanking the long metal spike out with both hands. The skin fell to the floor and she picked it up; then went back inside, shut the door, and locked it. *Fine.* She thought. *You want an enemy?* she addressed the unknown vandal, *You've got one.* She took the skin and threw it out the window, watching as it caught the breeze drifted away.

She decided to keep the spike, just in case whoever delivered it came back for another visit. She lay back in her bed, but this time sleep was a long time coming. Eventually Kiva drifted off, gripping the steel spike to her chest in her right hand.

The Harab Maneuver

Kiva awoke to a knock at the door. She glanced up at the window and saw the sun had well risen. The knock came again, this time with a voice, "Kiva, it's your father. Open up."

What's in my hand? She looked down and found that she was still clutching the steel spike.

"Coming."

She slipped it between the wall and the bedding and stood, hastily dressing herself.

Kiva reached the door, unlocked, and opened it.

"Hi Papa," she said quietly.

Her father stood before her for a brief moment, and she worried he might be angry with her. He then swept her up in his arms.

"Oh Kivanya. Little moon," he whispered.

She hugged him back, and strangely felt as if she were the one comforting him. He eventually released her, and they both stepped inside, closing the door.

"How are you doing?" he asked.

"I'm fine," she said, trying not to think about the skin stabbed into her door the night before.

"Are you sure? I can have them bring you more food. You look thin," he said, furrowing his brow and pinching at her arm.

"Papa I'm *fine*," she said, smiling more genuinely. "The only danger here is that I die of boredom."

"Good," he said, and his expression became more serious. "What were you *thinking?*"

"What? I—"

"You could have been killed! Those cliffs…the kiraeen… and that angry mob! If your brother hadn't been there—"

"Then I would have defended myself!" she asserted, her blood growing hot.

"That's not how it looked," he countered, frowning.

"I was caught off guard! It wasn't supposed to go like that."

"And how did you expect it to go? Did you think the windwalker sidi would simply appear and grant you membership in his sect? That he would change centuries of tradition, after being humiliated in front of everyone?"

Her father's words hit her like a clay brick. "He humiliated *himself!* It is not my fault the old qadim can't see beyond his own bias. The sect needs new windwalkers. It is not my fault Jado would cut off his nose to spite his face."

"Listen—"

"No *you* listen. You said it yourself, remember? 'The channels themselves would not exist, had the first few drops not dared to flow where none had before.'"

Her father pursed his lips together. He pushed a hand through his hair, looking away. "I did not mean for you—"

"But I did," she interrupted him again. "And here we are."

Her father sighed, and his expression changed from frustration to worry.

Kiva relented, reminding herself that he was not the

enemy. "This isn't just about me anymore, Papa."

"I know," he said, sounding even more troubled. "Your mother has told me some of what's going on."

"And do you support us?"

"Of course I support you! Both of you. But there are people out there—dangerous people—who do not. I worry for your safety, and for your mother's."

Kiva reached out and put a hand on his. "We will be fine, Papa. Look at our family. Two powerful stonemelters, and a *shadestalker*. None would dream of harming us." She again remembered the spike in her door, then banished the thought. "Plus, if we can get the council on our side, people will *have* to accept that things are changing."

After a brief pause, Kiva's father smiled. "You are just like her, you know."

Even just a few days ago, Kiva would have taken offense at being compared to her strict, overbearing mother. But now, she felt a newfound sense of pride.

"I may not be able to protect you at all times," he continued, "but I can at least help you defend yourself." He reached into his leather satchel and removed a bundle wrapped in cloth. "This is for you," he said, handing it over.

Kiva took the bundle and unwrapped it. Inside the faded purple cloth was a belt, festooned with ornate iron rings and rivets. At the center was a beautifully crafted khanjar sheath, and within it, an equally beautiful dagger hilt.

Kiva's eyes widened, and a smile spread across her face as she drew the dagger, admiring it. "It's beautiful," she said.

"I had planned on giving it to you once you'd chosen your sect."

Kiva felt tears welling in her eyes. She sheathed the dagger and wrapped her arms around her father. "Thank you," she whispered.

"You are welcome, little moon. Always."

A subtle knock came at the door, and he looked at her with regret.

"That would be the sect keeper. I am out of time," he said.

"Can't you stay a little longer?" she asked. "The days are so long."

"Mica had to pull many strings to get me up here at all. I don't want to cause trouble between him and his sect."

Kiva nodded. Things were delicate enough without any additional complication. "Will you visit again? Before the trial?"

Her father's expression fell, and she instantly regretted bringing it up. There was a good chance they'd never see each other again afterward.

"I will try," he said, before sweeping her up in another great hug. "Goodbye, Kivanya."

There was another knock, which they both ignored.

"Bye Papa," she said, squeezing him tight.

They parted, and after one last fond look, he opened the door and stepped out. Kiva locked the door, walked to her bedding and collapsed onto it, clutching the gift her father had given her. She began to imagine a life without her parents, or her brothers, and the pain she felt was nearly unbearable. *No,* she steeled herself against it. *I will not give up hope. Not yet.*

Kiva spent the rest of the afternoon going over the flight commands she'd learned the previous day, imagining herself soaring and diving as she pushed and pulled Zakai's harness. When that got old, she once again sat cross-legged on her bed, hands upturned on her knees, and closed her eyes. At first there was only the darkness of her eyelids. She slowed her breathing, felt the beating of her heart, and found a rhythm. Lights began dancing on the backs of her eyelids, like a murmuration birds flying in a swaying, undulating flock. The light grew brighter, and Kiva felt the wind touch her skin. The light became blinding, and by instinct she averted her gaze. Looking aside, she realized the light was the sun.

She was standing in the desert, in a place she did not recognize. She took in the vast expanse of sand and rock. Ominous dark clouds, as tall as the sky itself, were drifting toward her. It was a sight she had never seen before, and it brought with it a great foreboding. The thunderheads continued toward her at a speed she never imagined possible, until they blotted out the sun, casting her in shadow.

Something cold landed lightly on the back of her neck. Kiva reached back and found it wet. She looked at her fingers, which were covered in a thin sheen of red liquid. Another fell, and another, and another, until the storm clouds were upon her, releasing a torrential downpour of blood-red rain from the sky. Great bouts of thunder shook the ground, and bright bolts of energy stabbed down at the desert sand. There was nothing nearby that might have worked as shelter, so Kiva covered her head, attempting to shield her face from the torrent. The water fell so heavily she was driven to her knees. It painfully pelted her back as she willed it to relent.

After several long minutes, the hammering water abated. Kiva stood, wiping the red rain from her eyes and forehead.

The thunder clouds had passed, but she was still beneath a vast blanket of cloud cover. The once sandy ground had become muddy, stained red from the powerful downpour.

Two footprints materialized in the red mud several feet away, created by something unseen. Kiva tensed, reaching for her dagger. She found it at her waist, and took a guarding stance as whatever made the footprints took a step in her direction.

It took another step, and then another. Suddenly it was sprinting toward her. Kiva screamed a battle cry as it approached, slicing her dagger where the invisible assailant should have been. She struck only air. Her lungs were robbed of breath as it passed through her, and a disquieting shiver ran through her body.

She turned, gasping. A wave of hundreds, no, thousands of footprints sprinted away from her through the muddied sand.

Rising up from the desert before them were the great natural stone walls of Madina Basin.

I have to warn them!

Kiva sheathed her dagger and ran after the unseen army, toward the basin. With each step, her feet sank deeper into the crimson mud, until she was fighting through viscous liquid up to her thighs. She watched helplessly as the invisible attackers sped away.

No!

From above came the familiar screech of a kiraeen. Following the sound, Kiva found its dark form, contrasting against the cloud cover.

"Help me!" she shouted at the sky. "I have to warn them!"

It screeched again, and dove toward her. In a matter of seconds, it was nearly upon her, but had not slowed its descent. She realized then that the kiraeen intended to kill her.

Rooted to the spot in the thick mud, she did the only thing she knew how. She drew her dagger, preparing to fight, and likely die.

At the last second, the kiraeen spread its wings, extending its talons toward her. Kiva braced herself as it crashed into her at full speed.

Instead of pain, Kiva felt weightlessness. She opened her eyes and found herself back in her room, heart pounding rapidly in her chest. Taking several deep breaths, she attempted to calm herself, but even as her heart slowed to a normal pace, the sense of foreboding refused to depart. She had heard of mystics having visions, but she'd never experienced anything like it herself. *It seemed so real.*

A shiver ran down her spine, and she stood. Moonlight streamed in through the round opening in the wall. Kiva gasped. *The training!* She quickly grabbed her things and once again slipped out the window. She climbed to the top of the walls and saw several figures standing at the center of the clearing where she had met Jonah.

The moon was obscured by high clouds, casting everything in shadow. Kiva quietly crept forward to one of the stone formations surrounding the clearing. She watched a moment, and realized that none of the figures were moving, and many were strangely misshapen. She continued carefully forward, peering ahead, and understood that these were not people at all. They were training dummies, propped up and balanced on the stony ground.

Walking toward one of them, Kiva breathed a laugh. She grasped the white cloth draped over it, and lifted.

"You know—"

Kiva jumped and spun at the voice from behind.

She found Jonah looking at her with raised eyebrows. "Uzi might not appreciate you poking around beneath his robes." He attempted to suppress a smile and failed.

"Uzi? You named him?" she asked, smirking.

Jonah shrugged.

"Must you always sneak up on me like that?"

"Not always," he said. "Once you learn to sense with the wind as opposed to your eyes and ears, you will know I'm here without even turning around."

Windsense. Windwalkers were said to be so in tune with air currents, they could sense the contents of a room with their eyes closed.

"Will you teach me?" she asked.

"Yes," Jonah said, "but not tonight. Tonight, we focus on attack. With what's to come, we *must* be ready for anything."

"What's to come?" Kiva asked. "You mentioned something about signs the other day. What did you mean?"

Jonah's jovial smile faded. "Are you familiar with the Hikaya Sharun?"

"The fable of the sandshades?" Kiva recalled tales of the horrifying creatures that would rise up from the sand and cut your throat while you slept. Her older brothers loved to tell stories of them, tormenting her on nights they camped out in the desert.

Kiva nodded. She shifted uncomfortably as the uneasy feeling from her vision returned.

"The Sharun are real, and I believe they are returning."

Jonah adopted an uncharacteristically serious tone and began to recite,

*"The sands rose up and named us foe,
The plains wept blood where nothing would grow,
Upon dunes painted white, the Sharun take flight,
Reaping death and despair, in the absence of light."*

"But…those are just stories," Kiva insisted half-heartedly.

"Not stories," he said seriously, "Warnings."

"How so?" Kiva asked.

"Garra flowers," he answered simply.

"Garra flowers?" She furrowed her brow.

"Have you ever heard of the Mujdab Plains?"

Kiva thought for a moment. The name did sound familiar, but nothing came to mind. She shook her head.

"They are said to be the sacred place where our ancestors first set foot on this world. They are also completely barren—bereft of life. I've flown over them hundreds of times, and never seen so much as a blade of grass…until now."

"Garra flowers?" Kiva reasoned.

Jonah nodded. "By the thousands. Their crimson petals stain the once barren plains, as if it were weeping blood," he finished poignantly.

Kiva pursed her lips. "How do you know it's connected?

Couldn't that just be coincidence?"

"It could," he conceded, "but there's more. What do you think it means: *The sands rose up and named us foe*?" he asked.

Kiva thought for a moment, then took a guess. "Sandstorms?"

"Precisely," he answered. "Normally they only appear during the windy season, but I've encountered *four* in the past two moon-cycles, well into the withering."

"What about 'dunes painted white'?" she asked. "What does that mean?"

Jonah shook his head. "I'm not sure…"

Kiva frowned. The prospect of the storied shades returning chilled her to the bone.

"I've been reading the histories," Jonah explained. "The grandparents of our great grandparents endured decades of siege by the Sharun."

"The darktime," Kiva said, recalling the stories.

Jonah nodded. "I can't say for sure, but I fear we are heading for a second darktime," Jonah spoke with conviction, and a shiver ran down Kiva's spine.

"Have you told any of this to Jado?" she asked.

Jonah scoffed. "Many times. He refuses to listen… which is why we need to be ready," he said. "And that means learning how to fight."

Kiva sighed. "I already know how to fight," Kiva said, throwing an elbow back into the dummy, then following it up with her fist. It rocked on its stand, then slowly toppled over.

Kiva turned back to him, hoping he'd view her confidence as a challenge. She was far more interested in sparring with him than with the training dummies.

"With your limbs and fists, perhaps. But that is not what I had in mind." He tossed her the harness. Kiva caught it, and grinned.

Jonah put his hand to his mouth and whistled, and Kiva stepped into the harness, buckling it in front. Zakai arrived a moment later, buffeting them with wind as he set down.

"We're going to start simple. Talon attacks. Gain enough altitude to get a good speed up, then dive toward the dummy. Just before you are upon it, pull back on the harness, and Zakai will do the rest."

"Altitude, dive, pull back. Got it," Kiva said, barely masking her excitement.

"No aerobatics, understand? We are here to work."

"Understood," she said with a nod, but she was looking eagerly at Zakai.

He chirped an answer to Jonah as well.

Jonah raised an eyebrow at his kiraeen, then shook his head.

"Well? Go on then," he said, waving a hand.

Kiva approached, and Zakai brought his head toward her as he lowered himself. She placed a hand on his beak momentarily, then climbed up onto his back. He rose to full height, and she felt a wave ripple through his feathers. She clipped her harness to Zakai's.

"Oh, I almost forgot," Jonah said, rooting around in the pouch at his waist. He removed a small strap attached to something Kiva couldn't make out, and tossed it to her. She caught the strap, and the two glass lenses attached to it clanked together.

"Put those on. Can't hit a target if you can't see it."

Kiva nodded, and strapped the clear glass goggles over her eyes. She wrinkled her nose, trying to get used to the feeling of them on her face.

"Talon attacks, three targets. Got it?"

Kiva leaned forward and clipped in at the shoulders. "Got it," she responded.

"Zakai—"

"Zakai Yatir!" Kiva gave the command, and the great kiraeen sprung high into the air and flapped his wings. They soared out over the desert, and Kiva gave a gentle pull on the harness, sending Zakai into a climb. Rising higher into the sky, she grinned and breathed deeply. There truly was nothing that came even close to the experience of flight. With the moon shrouded in clouds, the desert appeared all shadows and darkness, far below. Kiva leaned gently to the left, and Zakai tilted his wings, circling around in a great arc.

Kiva found the basin, and scanned for the dummies. She squinted. They were so high now that she was having trouble pinpointing their departure point. A small fire bloomed to life atop the walls, and Kiva pointed Zakai toward it. She took a deep breath to calm her nerves, and pushed forward on the harness. Zakai gave a powerful sweep of his wings, then tucked them in as they dropped toward the flame.

The wind blasted by, and Kiva was suddenly grateful for the glass covering her eyes. They'd have been watering to blindness at this point. As they drew nearer to the flame, she could see that Jonah had placed it at the center of the circle. She picked out one of the shadowy target dummies and gently leaned toward it. Zakai responded, adjusting his descent toward the target.

As they closed in, Kiva's doubts began circling. *What if I wait too long to pull up? Zakai will fly us into the ground!*

They grew closer, and she could clearly see the details of the target. The stuffed ball of cloth that was its head. The white sheet covering its lumpy body, blowing in the breeze. They fell closer…closer.

We're going too fast! Kiva yanked back on the harness, and Zakai screeched, spreading his wings and extending his talons. He swooped back up with such force that her stomach dropped and her limbs felt twice their weight.

"*Trust Zakai, he will know…*" Jonah's voice carried faintly over the wind before fading.

"*Uff!*" Kiva muttered once they leveled out. "Sorry Zakai. Let's try again."

They once again climbed and curved around, taking aim. Kiva pushed on the harness and Zakai dove. This time they were perfectly lined up. Kiva just had to keep a handle on her nerves and trust that Zakai wouldn't fly them both into the ground at top speed.

The wind whipped by violently as they descended, a streak of black in the night. They drew closer, and a voice in Kiva's head began shouting that they would crash. This time she managed to ignore it. Resisting the urge to close her eyes, Kiva watched the target as they swiftly approached. Then, just before they'd have crashed into it, she pulled the harness, and Zakai spread his wings, extending his talons. She felt a dull thud as his powerful legs connected with the dummy, and they once again swooped up. The force was no less powerful, but Kiva was ready for it this time.

"Wooohoo!" Kiva cried. She heard Jonah cheering her on from below.

"Okay my friend, two more to go," she said with a grin. Once they climbed high enough, Kiva leaned back hard, and Zakai climbed vertically, then tipped back further until she was upside down. He continued the loop until they were angled toward the target, and Kiva applied pressure with her right leg, causing Zakai to roll so that she was once again upright.

They sped toward the target, and this time Kiva found it easier to ignore her fear. She even managed to throw her own weight into the impact, sending the dummy flying even farther than the last.

The third dummy fell just as spectacularly, after which they descended to the center of the clearing, landing gently. Kiva unclipped the front two rings of her harness and sat up.

Jonah walked up, wearing a small smile. He was holding the stuffed head of one of the dummies. "Well done, Kivanya."

Zakai chirped with annoyance.

"Yes, yes," he amended, "You too Zakai." He gestured for Kiva to hop down.

Zakai lowered himself, and Kiva unclipped the thigh harnesses and slid over the side. "Except I missed the first one," she said, annoyed at having let her fear get the better of her.

"It took me three tries to hit the target," Jonah responded. "Four to hit it squarely." He tossed the head to her.

Kiva caught it and looked over to where one of the dummies lay. It had broken apart after smashing into one of the rock formations across the clearing.

"If only we could take care of Jado so easily," Jonah muttered.

Kiva smiled, but it faded once she realized he wasn't joking. "Is he not your family?" she asked.

Jonah looked down. "No, not really. *Real* family doesn't treat you like a burden. If my father were still around, he would have talked some sense into Jado by now."

There was a pause, and Kiva tossed away the dummy's head, stepping closer to him. "Is it okay…I mean, can I ask—"

"What happened to my parents? Sure, I mean it's no secret," Jonah turned and walked toward a small stone formation, and sat, leaning up against it. Kiva followed, sitting cross-legged facing him. He uncorked a skin bloated with liquid, and held it out to her. Kiva took it and wet her parched tongue with the cool water before handing it back.

"I have no memory of my mother," he said, taking a drink and corking the skin. "Though my father used to speak of her bravery and kindness. She died giving birth to me. After that, my father decided to become a *tabie*—a man on the path to become a mystic." Jonah looked up at the sky. "He had the patience of a mountain, my father. It was infuriating!" Jonah smiled.

Kiva smiled back, waiting for him to continue.

"Anyway…" his smile faded. "When I was ten years old, my father had *the dream.*"

"The dream?" Kiva asked.

"Ahn Ket Suun," he said.

Kiva nodded. She had never been one for mysticism, but every last Sahra' was raised with the teachings of their desert deity.

"He became convinced that he had to go on a pilgrimage, deep into the Miralaja. When the time came, I begged him not to go. A large part of it was that I'd miss him, but mostly it was because I knew whose care I'd be under in his absence."

"Your Uncle Jado," Kiva said.

Jonah nodded. There was a long pause, and his eyes appeared far away.

"I can still remember so clearly the last time I saw my father." There was an expression of such sadness on his face, that Kiva had a powerful urge to place an arm around him.

"He had only a small satchel, a staff, and the clothes on his back. 'I will see you again' was all he said before he left me." Jonah did nothing to hide the resentment in his voice. "Turns out that was a lie," he said, looking away.

Kiva's heart went out to him. She understood at least the nature of his pain, having recently been faced with the prospect of losing her own family. Unable to restrain herself any further, she reached out and put a hand on his knee. "I am sorry," she said.

He turned his head to look at her with red-rimmed eyes. "It's fine," he said, forcing a smile. "At least one good thing came of it," he said, thumbing his leather windwalker vest. "Jado made it clear I would be challenging the windwalker sect following my sixteenth birthday…I might have done so anyway, but not having a choice made me furious."

"At least he wasn't the clayform sidi…you'd be making bricks and shakh pots all day." Kiva smiled, attempting to lighten his spirits.

Jonah let out a small laugh, and looked down at her hand on his knee, as if just now noticing it.

Kiva quickly removed it, and felt her face flushing. She cursed her skin for giving her away.

"I suppose you're right," he said. "Being a windwalker was the best thing for me. The solitude of the sky, the independence it affords. Did you know that windwalkers never marry? Once you've bonded and taken on your duties, there is little room for much else…which is fine with me," Jonah said a little too adamantly. "At least we'll never have to worry about being left behind, right?" He abruptly stood, and held out a hand to help her up.

She felt a pang of regret, but pushed it aside as she took his hand. Despite her efforts, a wave of tingling flowed through her skin at his touch. She stood as quickly as possible and released his hand.

It appeared that Jonah's puckish demeanor had fully returned. "There is one more exercise I'd like to try tonight. Normally, this wouldn't be attempted so early in one's training. Were you not such a quick study, and Zakai not so capable, I wouldn't suggest trying it. Even seasoned windwalkers can have trouble with the maneuver."

Kiva's interest was instantly piqued. "I'm in," she said. "What is it?"

"It is called the harab. It is an emergency escape maneuver, for use when a windwalker is in danger and needs to be elsewhere, as quickly as possible."

"How is it done?" Kiva asked.

"If executed improperly, it can result in injury, or even death," Jonah warned. "Rather than explain, I will demonstrate." Jonah walked toward the center of the clearing where Zakai waited patiently. He approached the kiraeen, and stood before him. Placing an arm on either side of Zakai's great head, he rested his forehead against the kiraeen's. It only lasted a moment, but Kiva understood there was something deep and profound about the gesture.

Jonah stepped back, placing his fingers to his mouth, and whistled. At the same time he made an upward gesture with his other hand, and Zakai leapt up into the air.

"Stand well back," Jonah warned, and Kiva took several large steps back.

Once she had cleared the area, Jonah glanced up to where Zakai flew. He cupped his mouth and shouted, "Zakai! Harab alan!" Jonah immediately turned and crouched, closing his eyes. Zakai screeched out and dove toward him.

Kiva's heart beat faster in her chest. Zakai was streaking down with incredible speed. He would reach Jonah in seconds. Kiva's expression changed from excitement to worry, as she remembered the dummy smashing into the nearby rock. *He is going too fast!* There was nothing she could do.

Suddenly Jonah burst up from his crouch, leaping into the air. His legs were straight and rigid, and his arms were extended out from his body. Zakai reached him at the exact moment that Jonah was fully extended. The kiraeen spread his wings wide, slowing his speed. At the same time, he swung his feathered legs forward, talons open wide. They closed around Jonah's arms, and in less than an instant, Jonah was flying forward through the air beneath Zakai. His body was prone, legs hanging straight back behind him. Zakai pumped his powerful wings, and they climbed upward, narrowly avoiding one of the rock formations.

Incredible! Kiva thought amid a swirling mixture of thrill and terror. They flew up into the darkness, out of sight. Kiva scanned the clouded night sky impatiently. A moment later she caught movement, and found Zakai's shape descending toward the clearing. As they grew closer, Kiva could see that Jonah had somehow moved onto the kiraeen's back.

Her mind suddenly flared brightly with the possibilities of flying without a harness. They glided in at great speed. Once they reached the clearing, Zakai spread his wings wide, quickly slowing them. They landed gently on the stone, and Kiva ran over.

"That was unbelievable!" she exclaimed, her eyes wide.

"With the right training, you too—"

"You were brilliant!" Kiva said, placing a hand to the side of Zakai's head.

Zakai chirped, rotating his head so that she could scratch the soft down beneath his beak.

Jonah cleared his throat. "You know, I was involved too, right?" he asked, raising an eyebrow.

"Oh yes, of course, *very* skillfully done," she said before turning her attention back to Zakai.

Jonah hopped down as Kiva once again congratulated the kiraeen on his excellent flying.

"Alright," Jonah said. "Your turn."

Kiva froze.

"Relax. You won't do it exactly like I did. For one, you only need to stand straight with your arms outstretched. Zakai will do the rest. Your only job is to keep calm, concentrate, and most importantly, *hold still.*"

Kiva swallowed.

What if I'm not ready? What if I flinch? Or Zakai misses and cuts off my arm? Or what if he drops—

Kiva forcefully cut off that line of thinking. *No. I am to become a windwalker, and windwalkers must conquer their fear.*

"Alright," she said, nodding.

"Good. As I said, you will stand at the center of the clearing with your arms outstretched. When you feel Zakai coming close, tense the muscles in your shoulders. This will prevent your arms from being pulled from their sockets, a *very* painful experience. Trust me," he said knowingly.

Kiva forced a nervous smile.

"Once he has you, allow your legs to drift back and make your body parallel to the ground. This will improve airflow, and reduce the weight Zakai must carry."

"And how am I to get onto his back up there?" she asked.

Jonah smiled. "That is a lesson for another day. For now, just focus on maintaining your nerve. It is no small thing, standing fast with a kiraeen bearing down on you."

"Right." Kiva clenched her fists to keep her hands from shaking.

"You'll do fine, just remember what I told you," Jonah said. He again whistled, making an upward hand motion, and Zakai lifted off, blasting them with air.

"Back straight, arms out," Jonah said, lifting her arms so that they were perpendicular to her body. He inspected her stance, and gave a nod of approval. "Remember," he said, backing away at a jog, "Keep absolutely still."

Right, she thought nervously. *Easy for you to say.*

She took a deep breath, fighting the urge to back out.

"Ready?" he asked from where he stood, thirty paces away.

"Ready." Kiva hoped he was too far to hear the waver in her voice.

"Zakai!" Jonah shouted. "*Harab alan!*"

SKYHUNTER

No backing out now, she thought, closing her eyes. The muscles in her shoulders would have been tensed, along with every other muscle in her body, even if Jonah hadn't suggested it. Right about now, Zakai would be streaking down through the sky toward her back, preparing to collect her in his massive, razor sharp talons. The same talons that could easily open her up from end to end in a single swipe.

Kiva felt her legs wobbling. It was so much worse not being able to see the kiraeen coming. Her fear returned with a vengeance, and she imagined the great beast bearing down on her. She experienced the sensation of slipping from his talons, and falling hundreds of feet to the rock and sand below. *I need more practice! I'm not ready!*

Kiva opened her eyes, and saw Jonah looking back at her. There was worry in his eyes. *He knows! He knows this was a mistake!* Panic threatened to take her, and she suddenly felt the great wind preceding the kiraeen. Kivanya's survival instinct took over, and she leapt aside.

"No!" Jonah's voice cried out, small and far away.

The pain was sharp and sudden. Kiva was yanked forward by her right arm. The ground sped by below her, as she was dragged across it. Zakai screeched out, and Kiva's eyes grew wide with terror. The pain in her shoulder was suddenly secondary to the tall stone formation they were speeding toward.

Kiva screamed out in pain as Zakai pumped his great wings once, twice, three times. They climbed until they were just high enough that her toes slid across the top of the stone. Zakai again screeched as they continued out over the drop. Hanging from a single dislocated arm, Kiva looked down at the shadowy desert floor, hundreds of feet below. She reached up with her free hand, grasping desperately at Zakai. A new pain erupted in her palm as it met the sharp end of his long, curved talon.

Zakai worked tirelessly, gripping her tightly. With each beat of his wings, brilliant red pain stabbed into her shoulder. The kiraeen awkwardly wheeled around, until they were back over the top of the basin walls. He quickly descended, and once they were several paces from the ground, he released her. Kiva fell, bracing herself, but never felt the punishing surface of the hard stone below. Instead, she landed on something softer. It grunted with the impact as she crashed to the ground.

Kiva lay there for a moment, in shock.

"Kiva!" Jonah spoke breathlessly. It was he who had broken her fall in an attempt to catch her. "Kiva," he gasped. He shifted out from under her, and she was suddenly aware of the immense, throbbing ache in her shoulder and sharp stinging laceration on her hand. Her back arched, and she cried out as nearly every muscle in her body tensed at the pain wracking her body.

"You're bleeding," he said with strained worry. He pulled a dagger from his belt, and quickly cut a strip of cloth from his pants.

"This is my fault," he said, pulling the cork from his waterskin and rinsing the wound on her hand. "I got too comfortable. The harab should never be attempted without a bonded kiraeen. I'm such a *fool!*" He gently wrapped her hand with the cloth.

Kiva groaned at the stabbing pain as he scooped her up in his arms and carried her over to one of the shallow caves surrounding the clearing. He gently set her down, and hot tears streaked down her face, though not from the pain.

"I'm sorry," she said through clenched teeth. "I panicked. I failed—"

"No," Jonah insisted. "This is my failure. You and Zakai were doing so well together, I thought…" He frowned, clearly distraught. "There is *no* substitute for a bond. I should have known."

Now that she was stationary, the pain in her arm transitioned from sharp stabbing to a dull throb.

Jonah leaned over her, his eyes stricken with concern. Despite the pain and trauma, Kiva thought she saw something in his eyes beyond an instructor's concern for his pupil.

"Can you forgive me?" he asked.

"There—*ah!*" Another pain shot through her arm as she tried to shift. "There is nothing to forgive," she finished. "Is Zakai alright?"

"You can ask him yourself," Jonah said, leaning back.

Zakai chirped from behind him, tentatively peering around.

"I think he might feel worse than either of us," Jonah said.

"I'm sorry Zakai. I should have trusted you…I just…"

Zakai cooed quietly, nudging her hand with his beak.

"It's not your fault," she insisted. "I'll be fine."

"Had you been bonded to Zakai, you would have known exactly where he was. Your connection with him would have allayed any anxiety. It was neither your fault, nor his." Jonah sighed deeply.

"Then I will just have to bond my own kiraeen," Kiva said, grimacing from the pain.

"First things first," Jonah said. "Your shoulder is dislocated. We need to re-set it. It will be painful at first, but once it's back in place the pain should diminish almost entirely."

"Let's get on with it, then," she said, grimacing.

Jonah nodded. "Here." He removed his vest, folded it, and placed it under her head. He then moved to her injured side and sat with his legs stretched out before him, feet resting against her torso. Jonah then gently grasped the wrist of her dislocated arm, which was resting on her chest.

Kiva grit her teeth, biting back the pain.

He slowly extended the arm to a ninety degree angle, so that her hand was resting on his lap. Kiva tried not to cry out, but was unable to remain silent.

"Ready?" he asked.

"Do it."

Jonah leaned back, bracing himself against her with his legs.

Kiva couldn't help crying out as her arm slid under the bone of her shoulder blade, and *thunked* back into its socket.

Red faced and panting, Kiva could feel the sweat standing out on her face. The pain in her shoulder was greatly reduced, just as Jonah had said it would be. He tenderly placed her arm back so it rested across her torso.

"I'm afraid you'll not be doing any climbing for at least a few days," he said. "The cut on your hand is shallow, but your shoulder will take time."

"What? No! I have to get back to my room," Kiva said sitting up. "Can you fly me down into it?"

"There's no safe way to pull that off, especially not in your current state."

"There has to be another way down…?"

"I am afraid not," he answered bluntly.

"*Al'ama*," she cursed. "What am I going to do? If they think I've escaped, they'll call off the trial. This will have all been for nothing!"

Jonah placed a hand to his chin. "I might be able to buy you some time…wait here. I'll be back in an hour."

"An *hour?*" she groaned, but he was already on his way out of the small cave. He returned a moment later with the torch he had been using to light the targets, and propped it between two stones beside her.

"I'll be back. You rest."

Kiva sighed and lay her head back on his folded windwalker vest.

She had no way to track the time, but when she heard him landing in the stone clearing outside, it felt far longer than an hour.

Moments later he rushed in, a stuffed satchel strung over his shoulder.

"Sorry that took so long," he said, crouching down beside her, pulling items from the overflowing bag. There were blankets, multiple jugs of water, clean bandages for her hand, dried aga strips wrapped in white cloth, and several other small necessities. He then lifted another strap she hadn't noticed over his head. It was connected to a hardened leather tube, which he pulled open. Inside were rolled up scripts. He handed the tube to her.

"What's this?" she asked.

"Reading material," he answered. "Windwalker history, philosophy, kiraeen care and temperament. That kind of thing. I thought this would be a good opportunity for you to catch up on the written part of your training."

Kiva nodded. "Thank you." She wasn't exactly thrilled at the prospect of reading all day, but it beat sitting in Mica's room, staring at the pattern on the rug.

"Were you able to do anything? You said you could buy some time?"

"I did have some success," he said cautiously, "Though it wasn't easy."

"Oh thank goodness," Kiva said. "How? What did you do?"

"I spoke with your mother and—"

"You did *what?*" Kiva asked, turning to him aghast.

"I spoke to your mother," he answered, as if he hadn't just committed a disastrous blunder. "Your father was there too of course. He is a *very* large man!"

Kiva palmed her forehead. "*Oh no.*"

"Listen," Jonah said, removing her hand from her face.

"It's fine. Your mother agreed to help. She will spend the next few nights in your room, accepting your meals from the keepers. She will tell them you have become ill, and that she is caring for you."

"*Uff*," Kiva exclaimed. "So they know you have been training me?"

Jonah nodded.

"My father must be furious," Kiva said hopelessly.

"On the contrary," he said calmly. "Of course, they were rather surprised to see me showing up at their home at such an hour…but once I told them of your success, and convinced them I wouldn't get their only daughter killed, they were both rather proud. Though your father did say that if anything happened to you, he would—"

"Proud…" Kiva repeated in disbelief. "They were proud?"

"Oh yes," Jonah nodded. "Here. Let's get that hand cleaned up."

Kiva held out her hand and Jonah took it, unwrapping the strip of cloth he'd cut from his pants.

"Did they say anything else?" she asked.

"They say they love you very much, and that they will try to come and see you again before the trial…once you're back in your room, that is."

Jonah poured cool water over her injured hand, and rewrapped it with clean bandages.

Kiva felt the knots in her stomach slowly unwind. She hadn't completely messed things up. The training would continue, and she still had a chance of being ready by the day of the trial.

"Your mother was actually quite glad for an opportunity to help," Jonah explained. "With the strike ongoing, she said it would give her something to do with all the extra time.

"Strike? What strike?"

"Oh that's right, you'd not have heard…" he trailed off.

"What? Out with it!" she pressed him impatiently.

"Nearly every last woman in the basin has stopped working, both in home and sect. They are demanding equal representation on the council of elders. The entire basin has ground to a halt. It is quite a sight to behold," he said with a grin.

Kiva smiled. Her heart filled with pride at the courage and strength of her mother, the weavers, and the women of the basin. She was proud to be a part of it.

Jonah unrolled her bedding and laid out the soft blankets and padding. Kiva shifted onto them using her sore, bruised limbs, and lay back.

"I've got to head home," he said.

Kiva's disappointment must have shown, because he quickly explained why.

"I would stay, but Jado is holding a sect gathering tonight. If I'm not there, he *will notice*."

"Of course, I should get some sleep anyway."

Jonah nodded and stood. "I've eastern patrol tomorrow, but I will try to stop by to see how you're doing. Tomorrow night, we will continue your training. Familiarize yourself with the scripts, specifically kiraeen origins."

"I will," said Kiva.

Jonah hesitated, and Kiva looked up at him.

There was shame in his eyes, which was quickly replaced with resolve. "I will do better by you, Kivanya Fariq. I swear it. On my bond." He turned and left the small cave, and Kiva watched as his dim form strode to the center of the clearing. He whistled, and Zakai landed beside him shortly after. Then, they were gone, and Kiva was once again alone.

She stifled a yawn, glancing at the nearby torch, still propped up between two stones. Several more lay nearby, unlit. She decided to leave it burning, closed her eyes, and attempted to sleep. After several failed attempts to get comfortable, she sighed and opened her eyes.

The tube of rolled up scripts was leaning against the cave wall nearby, and she idly reached for it. Squinting at the curving parchments in the dim torchlight, she leafed through until she found what she was looking for.

Kiraeen Origins

Klu albard, Ahn Ket Suun

The Sahra' home world of Tanusa, has fallen. Ahn Ket Suun, the Ancient One, leads his people through the great hollow between worlds. Within his immense body are housed those species of Tanusa worthy of preservation, including the kiraeen.

The bond between Sahra' and kiraeen began many centuries ago, before the exodus of our people. This Grand Rahil brought many changes, but the bonding between man and kiraeen was not one of them...

Kiva stifled another yawn. She'd already learned of the Grand Rahil—the exodus of the Sahra' from their ancient home—in her schooling. She understood the importance of knowing the histories, but it was over a thousand years ago. She flipped through the scripts, looking for something more interesting.

The Bonding

There is no bond more sacred than that of a windwalker and his kiraeen. To join with a skychaser is to forever change the reference point from which one frames his life. Once established, the bond is permanent, and nothing short of death will release it.

Kiva continued reading, absorbing as much as she could, when one section in particular caught her eye.

Once bonded, kiraeen skychasers must be kept separate from their female counterparts. Recognizable by their larger stature and bright red plumage upon the brow, female kiraeen are a male's greatest threat. Under normal circumstances, a female will keep her distance, and a bonded male will not seek her out. Should a female approach, she must be driven off without hesitation, lest the skyhunter destroy every last male kiraeen in the roost.

"Skyhunter," Kiva whispered, and a shiver ran down her spine. It was the same name driven to her mind by the kiraeen of her windwalker challenge.

A skyhunter is a female kiraeen, she realized. No wonder Jado had been so shocked to hear Kiva name herself one. She smiled, remembering the disbelieving expression on his face. She continued reading, lighting another torch once the first had burnt down. Soon that one too burned low, and the lettering grew blurred before fading into the darkness of dreams.

MEHALIA

"Kiva?"

Kivanya stretched beneath the covers of her bedding. Parchment rustled as it fell to the floor beside her. *Must have fallen asleep reading,* she thought.

"Kiva are you here?" Jonah's voice called, and he appeared at the opening of her small cave.

Kiva was genuinely glad to see him.

"How are you feeling?" he asked, approaching and crouching down beside her.

Kiva rolled her shoulder. It was sore, but nowhere near as bad as it had been the night before. "Better," she said, rubbing the sleep from her eyes and yawning. She turned to face him, and her eyes focused on his face.

"What's wrong?" she asked.

Jonah pursed his lips. "I have news…"

Kiva sat up. "What is it? What's going on?"

"The strike was a success. The council has agreed—women have won equal representation."

"*They did it?* That's wonderful!"

Jonah nodded. "Four men, and four women. The eldest mystic, Sidi Yehiel, will cast a final vote in the event of a tie."

Kiva breathed a sigh of relief. Her chances for avoiding exile had just improved significantly.

Jonah however, did not seem to share in her relief.

"What is it?"

"There's more," he said. "Sidi Yehiel has fallen ill. The healers say he will not last a week."

Kiva's heart leapt. "If Yehiel dies before the trial, his sister Suriel will become the eldest mystic."

Jonah only nodded, his expression serious.

"Don't you understand? This is *good* news! Suriel is far more likely to vote in our favor."

"There's more," he said flatly. "I overheard my uncle speaking with councilman Elam…"

"And?" Kiva asked impatiently.

"They are moving the trial forward, in order to ensure Sidi Yehiel's vote."

"Al'ahmaq!" she cursed, throwing a loose stone at the wall, then winced at the pain in her shoulder. "Can they do that?"

Jonah nodded.

"How far have they moved it? When will it be held?"

"Tonight," he answered gravely.

Kiva's face paled. *We're not ready.* "What are we going to do?" she asked. "I can't even climb back down to my room!"

Jonah took a deep breath. "From what I can see, we have but two options. I can have Zakai carry you down to the basin's entrance, and you can take your chances with the council as it now stands…With the new balance of men and women, your chances for avoiding exile are good. Better than good, I'd say."

"And what of becoming a windwalker?" she asked.

Jonah shook his head slowly. "Sidi Yehiel is old fashioned. He will not allow it."

Kiva's heart sank. She felt the burning of a fire, hot and defiant, kindle within her. "What is the other option?" she asked, leveling her gaze at him.

Jonah hesitated. "It's dangerous…I swore I would do better by you, Kivanya. I…"

Kiva's anger and frustration boiled up. She could feel the tirade forming on the tip of her tongue, but she forced it down. Jonah wasn't the one trying to clip her wings. He only wanted to keep her alive and safe…but ultimately it was her decision to make, not his.

"Jonah," she said, reaching for his hand. "It means a great deal to me that you care so much for my safety. But I need you to understand I am capable of making my own decisions. The responsibility, and the consequences are *mine* to bear, not yours."

He looked into her eyes, and as her heart called out to him, Kiva understood that there were some decisions in her life that would forever remain beyond her ability to control. Kiva asked him again, "What is the second option?"

Jonah sighed. "You bond your own kiraeen, today. If the entire council, plus Yehiel see what is possible, there's a good chance at least one of them will change their mind."

Kiva nodded. No woman had ever bonded a kiraeen before. She'd looked specifically for evidence of such in the scrips the previous night, and found nothing. Another impossible task…not that she'd been deterred by those in the past. But she was injured, and should something go wrong…

"What if they saw me flying on Zakai?"

Jonah shook his head. "I had considered that as well, but Jado would know, and he would tell the others that you were not bonded to him."

Kiva wracked her mind for another solution, but short of hastening Yehiel's death, couldn't think of one.

Kiva took a deep breath. "I will attempt the bonding," she said, getting painfully to her feet.

"There is a great deal you must know before—"

"You mean this?" she asked, picking up the script on bonding.

"Well…yes," he answered.

"I read through it last night. I think I understand how it works."

"And the consequences? The price?"

Kiva nodded.

"Then you know that the bonding process is an incredibly delicate one. It's not just the forging of the bond itself that poses a risk, but *how* it is executed."

"Right," Kiva said. "Push too hard, and you risk breaking the kiraeen's spirit."

"Correct, and your own along with it. Allow the kiraeen's raw, primal energy to dominate you—"

"And degenerate into a feral creature, untethered from rational thought and driven purely by instinct," Kiva finished for him.

Jonah nodded. "Forging the bond is all about balance. It is a dance between dominance and submission. A search for middle ground between the two. I do not control Zakai any more than he controls me."

"But he obeys your commands. You must have some control?"

Jonah shook his head. "No. He complies as a result of our shared purpose. If he chose to disobey my request, he would be well within his means to do so."

"When executed properly, a bond is comprised of loyalty, not control. A kiraeen bonded by control will obey your commands, but one bonded by loyalty will know when to ignore them."

Kiva furrowed her brow. *Why would you want your kiraeen to disobey?* "But the scripts said it was necessary to maintain control."

"Think of the scripts as a *guide,* rather than a set of rules. Not everything in them must be followed to the letter."

Kiva nodded.

"The balance struck at the time you solidify the bond will determine the permanent nature of your relationship. Would you spend a lifetime bonded with a loyal friend, or an obedient slave?"

"I think I understand," she said. She was both thrilled and terrified. Today was the day she would meet her kiraeen, and if all went as planned, bond the deadly predator. "I am ready," she said. "To the roost?"

"No. You remember what happened last time you were there. The way Zakai reacted to you on your first encounter…"

"Then how do you propose we do this? Do you know of another way?"

"Maybe…"

"Well?"

"The other night, we discussed the windwalker who attempted to bond a female kiraeen. Well, given the female we saw during your proving, I decided to dig deeper. What I found was…unexpected."

"What was it?"

"Kiva, you would not be the first woman to attempt bonding a kiraeen."

"What?" she asked, shocked. "Who was she? What happened to her?"

"The details were pretty thin," he said. "It was long before Jado. Back then Sidi Gidon led the windwalker sect. He had a strong and willful daughter, Mehalia, and he allowed her to give challenge. She passed the trials, and excelled in her training. She even managed to bond a kiraeen, for a time, but something went wrong."

Kiva frowned, leaning forward. "What happened?"

"Following a combat training exercise, the bond began to fail. The kiraeen became confused, and started lashing out at everything within reach. Two other windwalkers and a kiraeen were killed before it took Mehalia's life and flew full speed into a stone wall, breaking its neck."

Kiva was speechless.

"Apparently the bond was tenuous from the beginning."

"Has anything like this ever happened before?"

"Not that I could find. In the rare case of a failed bonding, a windwalker is either broken, or driven to madness."

Kiva took a deep breath, looking over Jonah's shoulder to

the cave opening. "Did the histories say *why* something like this could have happened?"

"They do."

"What do they say?"

"After the incident, Sidi Gidon stepped down. He was blamed for the disaster, and accused of bringing shame to the windwalker sect."

"That explains why Jado refuses to entertain the idea of a female windwalker," Kiva realized aloud.

"The histories were written by those who had succeeded Gidon. *They* claimed the kiraeen refused to accept Mehalia because she was female."

"I see," Kiva said, unconvinced. "And what do you think?"

"I think they are right…at least in part."

Kiva's anger flared up, but instead of berating him, she held her tongue and waited for him to finish.

"I think the reason Mehalia failed was because she was female…and her kiraeen was male."

Skyhunter. The word once again echoed in Kiva's consciousness, and her anger dissolved. "You think I should bond a female kiraeen."

"None have succeeded in doing so before, but all of those who attempted were men."

Kiva's mind cast back to her trials. The imposing kiraeen, larger than the others with red feathers atop her head. Kiva could almost feel the unbridled primal energy flowing off her in waves. What Jonah said made sense, and his idea felt somehow *right*. But there were still problems.

"Say you're right, and I must bond a female for this to

work. How would we even go about finding one?" she asked.

"I have been considering this idea for the past few days, and when not on patrols, I have tasked Zakai with seeking one out. Unlike the males, females roost alone. Zakai has found one such roost in the mesas to the southwest."

Kiva sat for a long moment, considering.

"It won't be easy…especially not in your state," Jonah warned.

She knew all too well how right he was. The first flight, essential for sealing the bond, would be turbulent at best. Kiva considered resuming life as normal with her family in the basin. She tried to picture herself issuing a challenge to the weaver sect, finding a husband…but the illusion wouldn't hold. There was no going back.

"It's not too late. You can still face the trial as is. They will not exile you…especially if you admit fault—"

"No," she said. "I have chosen my path. I will not abandon it now."

Jonah looked at her. In his eyes she saw respect, worry, and she again wondered if there might be a hint of something more.

Kiva stood, and he rose as well.

"I will have Zakai take you to the female's roost, after which he will return here to me. It will be too dangerous for him to remain. If there were more time, I'd have you wait for him to bring me to you…but the trial is in a matter of hours. Once you've bonded your kiraeen, you will need to go directly there. If you fail to arrive, you will be found guilty, regardless of votes."

"Of course," Kiva said. "I understand."

They walked out of the cave into the clearing. Kiva's joints ached, but her bruised limbs were nowhere near as painful as they had been the day before.

Jonah whistled twice, and Zakai sprung from his perch and glided down toward them. Kiva watched him descend, while Jonah checked the straps of her harness. "Not too tight?" he asked.

"No, that's good thank you."

Zakai landed beside them in a gust of wind. Jonah stood before Kiva, and she could tell he was questioning his decision to send her off.

"I will be fine," she insisted. She did her best to bury the anxiety twisting in her belly.

"I should come with you—"

"No. You said yourself, you wouldn't get there in time," she argued.

"But if you're injured—"

"If I don't return for the trial, then you may come for me…but if you risk yourself or Zakai, so help me I'll—"

"Okay," Jonah agreed, holding up his hands. "Alright, I'll await you in the basin below." He then placed his hands on her shoulders, and faced her calmly. "You can do this. It's time to change what it means to be a windwalker."

Kiva nodded, and Zakai lowered himself. She grasped the harness with her bandaged hand and winced, pulling herself up. Shifting her weight, she began to latch the thigh clips of her harness; then decided not to. If she was going to ride her own kiraeen with no harness, she would have to get used to it.

"Oh," Jonah exclaimed, "I almost forgot." He reached into his satchel and pulled out a bundle of brown leather straps. "It's a bonding harness. You'll need it for your first flight."

"Thank you," she said, taking the harness. With no buckles or clips, it was far simpler than the one on Zakai. She bundled it into a small bag over her shoulder. "For everything."

This is it, Kiva thought. She would bond her kiraeen, or die trying.

She took one last look at Jonah, then turned her gaze toward the clear blue sky.

"Zakai, *yatir!*" she shouted, and he sprung forward through the air, climbing skyward.

The Bonding

Yellow rays of light shone through the thin, scattered cloud cover. Zakai hit a thermal updraft—the result of a dry patch of ground baked all day under the sun—and was pushed upward. They quickly climbed, and were soon gliding across the desert, high above the tops of the jagged, rocky buttes.

Once they'd reached cruising altitude, Kiva sat up straight and closed her eyes, breathing deeply. The black headscarf her mother had given her trailed behind, tucked into her tunic, and the dagger from her father rested at her waist. The air cooled the sweat on her brow, and she pictured the female kiraeen—the skyhunter—in her mind. She again opened her eyes, reached back, and ran her hand along the leading edge of Zakai's great wing.

Far off in the distance, the blurred line of a sandstorm swept across the pocked, reddish-brown landscape. Kiva frowned. *A bad omen. Well,* she reasoned, *at least I'm not down there.*

Zakai tilted his wings, adjusting their course, and Kiva looked forward. Along the horizon an imposing mountain range climbed to dizzying heights. It was the same one she'd seen from atop the buttes she used to scale with Mica and

Amir. Running along their base was a broad strip of dark green plant life, climbing partway up.

Directly below, the dry, rocky desert landscape began transitioning to great, rolling sand dunes. The aureate afternoon light turned the hills of sand into rippling waves of molten gold.

Nearly an hour had passed before Zakai began to descend. Kiva had never seen this part of the desert before. It was beautiful, but had she been down on the ground, she'd have felt unsettled and exposed amid so much sand, and so little stone in which to seek cover.

Zakai tilted his wings, and they curved south toward a towering wall of stone. The enormous natural formation climbed up out of the sand, presenting its flat topped surface to the sun. Judging by Zakai's angle of descent, Kiva guessed that their destination would not be a skyward roost, but something else entirely.

The details of the craggy stone wall grew clearer as they approached. Dark, irregular shadows marked openings in its face. It was toward one of these that Zakai flew, adjusting his feathers to account for the warm draft of air.

Kiva held his harness with one hand, her head raised high to get a good view of their destination. A few more minutes, and they were on fast approach toward a large, darkened opening. It was one of the bigger crevices, narrowing to a peak thirty paces high. Zakai tilted his body back, flapping his wings to bleed off speed as he descended onto a rocky perch, just below the opening. He then turned his long neck back and looked at her with one eye.

Kiva met his gaze. "Thank you, my friend."

Zakai let out a low, warbling whistle in a descending tone. Despite their lack of bond, Kiva understood exactly what he meant. "Don't worry about *me*," she said, smiling. Kiva slid over his side, carefully finding her footing on the precarious protruding rock. One slip, and she'd be falling long enough to count to one-hundred. "It's the skyhunter who should worry," she said with a grin.

Zakai gave an uncharacteristically quiet chirp, and lifted off, wheeling around back toward the basin. *Goodbye, my friend.*

Kiva turned to face her fate. The cavern before her was dark and still. No sound or movement came from inside. Either the skyhunter was deep within, or she was out on the hunt. Kiva considered what she would do if the kiraeen were to arrive this very second. Remembering the swooping talon attacks she and Zakai had performed, she opted to take her chances *inside* the cave.

Kiva lowered herself from the perch, onto a narrow ridge that ran along the wall below the cavernous opening. With her back flat against the wall, she cautiously side-stepped along it. Once directly below the cave, Kiva shifted her body around and pulled herself up into it. She paused, listening closely. The only sound was the gentle, near constant breeze.

Pulling her shemagh over her head, she stepped forward on the rocky, uneven floor, peering into the darkness beyond. She continued as far as she dared, just beyond the edge of light cast by the afternoon sun.

Kiva stood a moment, listening and watching. *This is it,*

she thought. Heart pounding, she took a powerful stance and readied herself.

With a deep breath, she announced her presence, "I am Kivanya Raisel Fariq, windwalker of Madina Basin!"

There was only silence, and she continued, "Show yourself, skyhunter, and heed the call of she who would bond you." They were the same words spoken for the male bonding ceremony, changed slightly for her purposes.

There was only more silence, and after several tense seconds, Kiva slouched. *Must be on the hunt,* she concluded. Turning back toward the entrance, she stepped into the light. The view was spectacular. To her left, the light cloud cover had begun to glow bright orange as the sun made its way across the sky, toward the great mountains. Straight ahead, the desert stretched out, seemingly forever. The hazy outlines of long, flat mesas gave shape to the horizon. To the right, the skyline faded to a deep, rich cobalt. Kiva lowered herself to a crouch, basking in the natural glory of this world. As beautiful as it was, she was unable to fully lose herself in the view. If the kiraeen didn't soon return, she would miss her trial altogether.

Staring out across the silky dunes, Kiva watched, and waited. A gentle draft of wind blew, but there was something odd about it. Her brows knitted together. The draft had come from behind.

She stood, spinning around and peering into the darkness. Two small, orange lights stood out amid a sea of black. *She's been watching me the whole time.* Neither of them moved. Kiva stood in ready stance; the kiraeen remained in the shadows, watching.

Kiva reached out to the creature, as she had with Zakai. Slowly, the great kiraeen stepped forward, her eyes steady as she moved. Kiva swallowed, and redoubled her efforts. The kiraeen continued forward until it was just beyond the light—a large, shadowy figure of razor sharp talons, rock hard beak, and great, powerful limbs.

"*Sahl*," she said gently, and the kiraeen screeched a challenge. The sound echoed painfully in the enclosed space, causing Kiva to duck her head.

The kiraeen screeched again, and Kiva began to sweat. It didn't appear to be affected by her attempts to connect with it.

I have to calm it down, she thought, fighting to keep her hands steady.

The kiraeen stepped forward menacingly, abandoning the shadows. Kiva's pulse quickened. This close, the kiraeen's enormous size was even more pronounced. She was nearly twice as large as Zakai. The creature's feathers ruffled in a wave across her body as she stalked forward on her winged front limbs. Her onyx beak slightly parted, she crouched low, tail whipping around behind.

"*Sahl, sadiq,*" Kiva said, trying to keep her voice calm.

The kiraeen's tail fanned open at the tip displaying a pattern of red and black feathers, dancing in graceful figure-eights overhead.

Not good, she worried. Kiva's first instinct was to reach for her dagger, but instead she slowly took the rope harness from the pouch at her belt. She ignored the kiraeen's tail, and maintained steady eye contact.

"*Ainhasar—*"

The kiraeen burst forward with all of her strength. There was no time to think. Kiva leapt into the air. She spun her body sideways to avoid the head, and blindly threw the harness. The kiraeen's beak snapped shut through open air as it passed, and Kiva was suddenly jerked forward. The pain in her injured shoulder was immediate and severe, but she held on. Somehow, the harness had found the kiraeen's neck as it passed.

Kiva was dragged along the rocky floor of the cavern as the kiraeen flew forward. The creature landed at the entrance, and pushed off with powerful rear limbs. In seconds, the ground disappeared. Kiva found herself dangling from the harness, hundreds of feet above the sandy desert below.

She clung desperately as the kiraeen pumped her powerful wings, attempting to shake her loose.

Kiva's grip was worsening. With her other hand, she reached desperately for the harness, and missed. She now hung precariously from the strap, clinging with only three of her five fingers. The kiraeen jerked her head upward, and the harness was ripped out of her hand.

Kiva gasped. She was falling. *No!* she thought desperately. The air rushed past her, and the great kiraeen screeched victoriously from above. *I've failed.* Kiva's heart was pounding explosively in her chest. She closed her eyes. This falling sensation. It was an echo of one she'd experienced before.

Windfaith.

This time, there would be no water to break her fall. It didn't matter. If she was going to die, she would die in the arms of the wind. Kiva spread her arms and legs wide, mimicking the kiraeen's gliding form, and descended toward the desert floor.

As the features of the ground rushed toward her, growing larger and more defined, Kiva thought of her family. *I am sorry Mama. I wish I could have helped.* Her one comfort was knowing her parents and brothers were resilient. They would weather the storm of her death, and continue on.

Kiva heard another screech close by, and she squinted, looking around with watering eyes. A black shape dove toward her. Kiva's first thought was that the skyhunter had come to finish her off before she hit the ground. But as it drew near, she realized it was too small to be the female. The kiraeen slowed, matching her speed.

"Zakai!" she cried out with joyous surprise as he shifted below her. Kiva grasped his harness, and felt her weight rest against him as he began climbing upward. Kiva smiled, unspeakably grateful for the feeling of his soft feathers against her cheek. "Thank you," she whispered.

An outraged screech pierced the air above. Kiva looked up and saw the female kiraeen diving toward them. "*Yatir! Yatir!*" Kiva urged. Zakai pumped his wings with all his strength, but it was no use. Had Kiva not been on his back, he might have out-flown her, but as it was, the skyhunter was dropping toward them too quickly.

Zakai knew he was outmatched. As she approached, he turned mid air to face her, shielding Kiva with his body. Talons held forward, Zakai screeched as the female crashed into them. Kiva's vision was filled with a swirling mass of black feathers and snapping beaks. They tumbled through the air, falling awkwardly toward the ground. Suddenly, they broke apart, each swooping back up toward the sky. Kiva could feel that Zakai was no longer flying with his usual vigor. There was very little chance they could endure another attack.

Kiva leaned forward and placed her hand on Zakai's neck. "Listen my friend," she shouted over the wind. "You must out-climb her!"

Zakai chirped, changing course. The air temperature felt suddenly warmer, and they began quickly climbing. *A thermal!* Kiva thanked the sun, and looked back. The female kiraeen was closing the distance between them, but being smaller and lighter, she and Zakai climbed faster.

"Just a little higher!" she urged. Zakai beat his powerful wings, and they soared up on the warm air.

Another backward glance showed the female kiraeen not far behind. She too had reached the thermal and was quickly on the rise.

"Now!" Kiva shouted, pulling back hard on Zakai's harness. His response was quick, but still slower than usual. He climbed vertically, then tipped backwards. Kiva looked up toward the ground, and saw the skyhunter approaching. Rather than fear or apprehension, she felt a fire growing in her belly. *Keep your claws off of him!*

Kiva released her grip on Zakai and fell, rolling to face down as she did. The female kiraeen arrived below her, and Kiva crashed onto her back, then nearly slid off. With one hand on the loose bonding harness, and another clutching a fist full of feathers, Kiva pulled herself up. Once she had both hands on the straps, she redoubled her grip, twisting the straps around her forearms.

"Enough!" she shouted, pulling hard on the tough leather.

Other than an annoyed screech, the kiraeen gave no sign of obeying. She continued beating her wings, relentlessly pursuing Zakai. Kiva could see now why he had lost some of his speed and control. Several feathers had been pulled out from his left wing.

"I said *stop!*" Kiva shouted, but it wasn't doing any good. She was once again turned upside down as the kiraeen followed Zakai, who was now diving toward the ground.

She'll be on him in seconds.

Kiva felt a sudden sense of calm, and she understood what she had to do.

Despite bearing a rider, the skyhunter ignored Kiva for the most part. She'd identified Zakai as the greater threat. She was wrong.

Kiva unwrapped her right arm from the harness, and pulled her dagger from its sheath. They were in a steep dive behind Zakai. His tail was inches from the skyhunter's beak. Kiva steeled herself, and raised the dagger.

The female suddenly broke off, swooping back up away from Zakai. The force of the sudden climb pressed Kiva hard against the kiraeen's back. After several long seconds, she broke off the climb and spun, rolling and flipping through the air. Kiva had no choice but to sheathe her dagger in order to keep from being thrown off. She grasped the harness with both hands and squeezed her thighs tight.

The kiraeen continued to fly wildly, twisting, turning, and diving with all her strength. Kiva maintained her grip, though her shoulder screamed, and the sore muscles of her legs threatened to relax. The strain of holding so tight for so long had taken its toll. Kiva was moments away from complete exhaustion when the kiraeen began to slow. She was no longer rolling and diving, and the beat of her wings felt decidedly heavy.

With a defeated chirp, the exhausted beast spread her wings wide, gliding down toward the desert sands. Kiva was panting; both physically and mentally exhausted. The blessedly smooth flight meant she could finally relax her muscles. Now she just had to stay conscious.

The sandy ground drew closer. They were heading toward the ridge of a great dune. The kiraeen hadn't made any effort to slow her forward speed. It occurred to Kiva that she no longer had the strength. Kiva watched the ground, which was now speeding by only a few paces below. They sank down further, and Kiva ducked her head.

They were suddenly and abruptly slowed as they made contact with the long ridge. Sand exploded into the air on either side as the kiraeen slid forward on her belly, while Kiva clung to her back. After a few seconds that felt like minutes, they slowed to a stop.

Kiva unwrapped her arms from the harness and rolled off the great beast. She landed on her back, staring up at the sky. Both of them lay there panting heavily, too drained to move.

Remember, Kiva's exhausted mind grasped for the coherent thought. She closed her eyes, concentrating. What was I supposed to remember?

She opened her eyes, and her brows furrowed... *The trial!*

Kiva rolled over and pushed herself up with shaky arms,

drawing on a reserve of strength even she hadn't known she possessed. Beside her, the kiraeen lay in the sand, wings resting limply at her sides. Kiva slowly sat up, and a moment later managed to get to her feet. With slow, shaky steps, she trudged around to where the kiraeen's head lay upon its outstretched neck, resting in the sand.

The skyhunter's eyes were open, and she watched Kiva with unsettling alertness.

"I am Kivanya Raisel Fariq, windwalker of Madina Basin," Kiva breathed from her dry, scratchy throat. "Show yourself, skyhunter, and heed the call of she who would bond you."

Kiva fell to her knees before the creature, and once again reached out with her mind. The kiraeen's eyes narrowed, then grew wide. Her pupils dilated, and Kiva felt her own relax.

She soon found herself drifting through the ether of the kiraeen's consciousness. Like Zakai, the skyhunter's mind was filled with threads of animal instinct, pulled taut by an inborn drive for survival. There were far more here, however, than within Zakai.

Kiva's attention was drawn by movement in the distance. She sensed a powerful pulsing energy, growing stronger by the second. This was it. The kiraeen's *rüh*. Only instead of her seeking it out as the scripts instructed, it was fast approaching her.

It drew closer, emanating power that flooded over Kiva in immense waves. It shone through the threads of instinct, sending shafts of light through the ether. Kiva steeled herself, and the power came crashing into her.

And so began the dance. Kiva was immediately

overwhelmed by the powerful onslaught, but she held on, refusing to be taken without a fight. Pushing back with all of her being, Kiva fought to keep the madness at bay. She understood right away that there would be no risk of breaking this kiraeen's indomitable spirit. The best she could hope for would be a balance in which she could maintain her humanity.

Kiva concentrated, working to keep herself centered as she braced against the sandstorm of the kiraeen's rüh. The skyhunter pushed, but Kiva was ready for it. She waited for the mental assault to abate, then shoved back with all her strength. It was working. If she could hold her ground, she would soon strike a balance. The kiraeen lifted its head and screeched, pushing her back with all its strength. Sweat stood out on Kiva's face, and a drop of blood trickled down from her left nostril.

The kiraeen's force relented for a split second, and Kiva shoved with the last of her strength. A balance was struck. Kiva and the skyhunter's rüh were split perfectly down the center. Kiva quickly leaned forward, grasped the skyhunter's great beak in both hands, and pressed her forehead to the kiraeen's. She had the strange sensation that her mind was no longer fully her own, and she collapsed back into the sand, staring up at the sky.

The bond was forged.

A wave of cold rolled over her, and white ash began falling from the sky. One floated gently down and landed on her nose. *Cold,* she thought, realizing that the ash was not ash at all, but frozen drops of rain.

The Trial

Ismaela Fariq looked nervously to the sky, gauging the position of the late afternoon sun. *Where is she?* Her daughter had been stowed away atop the walls of the basin, but now the farce would have to end. *What has that fool boy done with my daughter?*

The crowd, which had been clamorous, now mumbled idly, awaiting a verdict that at this point, seemed inevitable. Kivanya had been due nearly an hour ago, and Ismaela could stall no longer. If Kiva didn't soon show her face, the verdict would be guilty by default.

Ismaela looked out over the crowd from behind the seven stone benches of the council. An eighth bench had recently been added, though it was made from the dried, gnarled wood of the chitalpa tree—a temporary measure until another stone bench could be crafted. Hundreds had gathered to witness the trial, and support, or oppose Kivanya. Nearly all women wore black headscarves, embroidered with the kiraeen symbol Ismaela had contrived. Some of the men wore them as well, including her husband, Haruk. The council members spoke in hushed tones at the far end of the qarar—a low shelf of stone that served as a stage for public hearings.

Netaniah—council elder, and leader of the weaver

sect—glanced to Ismaela from across the stage, her expression dark. She had been convening with the other elders as time ticked away. They eventually broke off, each finding their seat on the stone council benches, except for Netaniah. She approached Ismaela, wearing regret upon her face.

"I am sorry," she said. "The council members are decided. They will delay no longer. If Kivanya can not reveal herself, then we are powerless to help her."

Ismaela felt her hopes beginning crumble. *She's coming! She has to,* she thought, but the only outward indication she gave was a curt nod.

The sympathetic look on Netaniah's face hurt more than any of the insults Ismaela had endured from the opposition over the past week. That look of pained concern meant one thing—it was done. Suddenly all of their work uniting the women of the basin, their exuberant victories—including council representation—meant nothing. *I'm going to lose my little girl.* Ismaela's eyes welled up, and Netaniah put a hand on her shoulder. "I am sorry," she said again, before turning to take her seat among the other council members.

Ismaela cast a venomous look toward Jado, before turning forward to scan for signs of her daughter.

The crowd quieted as word spread that a verdict would be forthcoming.

Senior councilman Daivari stood and stepped out toward the center of the stage. At one time, his ceremonial white robes would have ended just above the ground. But the years had taken their toll, and the last few inches now dragged at his shuffling feet.

Everyone watched his gradual procession with growing anticipation.

Kiva, where are you?

He reached center stage, and lifted his bald head. "People of Madina Basin," he called out in a powerful voice. "You bear witness to the trial of Kivanya Raisel Fariq, accused of violating sect enrollment protocol, trespassing on sect land, public disruption, and being accountable for the death of a kiraeen belonging to the windwalker sect."

The crowd murmured in surprise at the last charge. Ismaela caught the comments of those surrounding the stage.

"Hah! A small girl, killing a kiraeen? Preposterous!"

"More of Jado's lies!"

"That girl is a menace!"

"Exile the blasphemer!"

Ismaela furrowed her brows. This charge was not among those she'd known were coming. There was no way Kiva could have killed a kiraeen, at least not by herself. What was more likely was that Jado piled on the false charge to ensure a severe punishment.

Daivari lifted his palms, gesturing for quiet. After a few moments, the agitated crowd once again hushed.

"Our laws dictate that the accused *must* appear before the council, or face the full extent of punishment for the alleged crimes."

Ismaela's gut clenched. *Kivanya...*

The old man took a ragged breath.

"By the obligations of the council, and the sanctity of Sahra' law, I hereby pronounce Kivanya Raisel Fariq, gui—"

A shrill screech interrupted the verdict, and a shadow, dark as night was cast upon Daivari, turning his white robes gray. He lifted his balding head skyward. His mouth fell open, and his eyes grew wide.

Ismaela followed his gaze, and the breath escaped her lungs.

Soon those in the crowd were shielding their eyes as they pointed up, shouting in surprise.

Ismaela watched in awe as the great, dark shape of a ki-raeen descended into the basin.

Temperance

Kiva clung to the back of her newly bonded kiraeen. She was still growing accustomed to the strange new sensation of sharing her consciousness with another. The creature had no name recognizable in Sahra' language. Unlike Kiva's people, the kiraeen did not give names passed down from parent to child, but rather their names were derived from the world around them. When Kiva first enquired as to the kiraeen's, her response was a projected scene in which a halo of soft moonlight reflected across a thin layer of clouds high above the desert floor. Kiva searched herself for a name that might closest represent the vision, and chose Noor.

Noor also desired a kiraeen name for Kiva. After a moment of deliberation, a new vision was projected into Kiva's consciousness. It was a desert sunrise. The condensation that had gathered in the night was evaporating into a gentle haze, blanketing the land. To Noor, Kiva was the mist, which despite being burned away each morning, persisted, returning the following night.

Kiva approached their bond with great will and purpose. Rather than attempting to dominate, she engaged Noor with respect, and Noor returned the sentiment. Both understood that they would never again be adversaries. Each had proven herself worthy of the bond, and accepted it as such. Kiva marveled at the powerful instinctive protectiveness she felt for Noor. If their relationship was anything like the one between herself and Zakai, it would only grow stronger.

Who is this Zakai? Noor thought jealously.

Kiva smiled to herself. *Jonah's kiraeen. He is a friend.*

The same that brazenly trespassed on my perch? Noor ruffled her feathers. She was having a hard time accepting that males could be considered allies. *He has already felt the edge of my beak, I welcome another chance to clip his wings.*

Stop that, Kiva scolded, half amused by Noor's vigor. *Zakai is a friend. He saved my life, and he will not be harmed.*

Noor didn't respond, but Kiva got the distinct impression that she was brooding.

There, Kiva thought, pointing. *Madina Basin.*

You are sure you wish to do this? Noor asked. *The ground-dwellers will not be pleased at my presence in their den.*

It is the only way, Kiva answered. *Don't worry, none will have the courage to attack you.*

Noor gave the kiraeen equivalent of a scoff. *I do not fear being attacked.*

Kiva's kiraeen sensed her apprehension.

Should any touch you, they will touch nothing else ever again, Noor thought, snapping her beak.

They would be foolish to try, Kiva thought. On that point, they were in complete agreement.

Noor pumped her wings, driving them forward through the air at great speed.

Kiva looked ahead, and blinked. In addition to the

instinctive, emotional connection she shared with Noor, came something more. Something unmentioned by Jonah, or any of the scripts. Up ahead, Kiva could actually *see* the wind curling into graceful eddies. To the east, a great rising column of air pushed its way up from the rocky ground, and far above, a steady stream of wind rushed northward across the sky. Noor called it windsense, and considered Kiva's unfamiliarity further evidence of the superiority of her species.

Kiva blinked again, concentrating on tuning out the additional visual stimulation. They soon soared over the southwestern wall of the basin. At the northern side, several kiraeen took flight, and Kiva was able to spot riders on their backs. Her improved farsight was another gift attributed to the bond. She wondered if Noor had benefited from any of her traits.

There, Kiva thought, relieved. *Do you see the crowd of people?*

I see them, Noor acknowledged.

Kiva sensed a growing apprehension within Noor.

You must not attack any of them, Kiva warned. *If this is going to work, we will need to be windwalker and skyhunter, not young girl and deadly kiraeen.*

Noor grudgingly agreed. *But if they strike first…*

Kiva didn't have to answer. Anyone foolish enough to attack a windwalker and her kiraeen would deserve the consequences. She just hoped none of the other windwalkers would follow her down into the basin. They were forbidden to do so, but these were unusual circumstances.

Down below, upon the stone shelf of the qarar, stood a

single figure. The seven other council members sat on their benches, behind.

They're delivering the verdict! Quickly! Kiva urged.

Noor's beak parted and she let loose a piercing screech, diving toward the stage with tremendous speed. The council members all stood, and those in the crowd pointed as Noor streaked down toward them.

A mere several feet from the ground, Noor spread her wings wide, catching the wind and rapidly slowing them before smoothly setting down before the bewildered councilman at the center of the stage. Kiva recognized him as sidi of the stonegrower sect.

Not a soul spoke, and an eerie silence settled over the entire proceeding.

Noor spread her wings, tail whipping wildly behind, and lowered herself. Kiva slid over the side, and approached councilman Daivari. He was still staring at the over-sized kiraeen sharing the platform, when Kiva reached him.

"I apologize for my late arrival," Kiva said calmly. The silence held, and she leaned over in an attempt to draw Daivari's gaze away from Noor. "I have come to stand trial." Kiva felt invigorated. It was no longer just her own boldness that drove her, but the razor sharp predatory awareness of her kiraeen.

Daivari finally noticed her standing before him, and looked to her with brief surprise. "Yes. Of course—"

"What have you done?" It was Jado's voice that cut the silence. He was walking forward. "Blasphemous girl! You would bring a female, *here?*"

Noor turned her attention to him, and the look she gave froze him on the spot.

Kiva, being privy to Noor's desires, gave her a warning glance. *No violence.* Kiva turned then not to Jado, but the crowd.

"*Tradition* says that women are forbidden from joining the windwalker sect. That we lack the strength to complete the trials…the *will* required to bond a kiraeen." She paused, and the crowd began to murmur now that the initial shock had worn off.

"And yet I have done *both*." Kiva gestured to Noor.

"This is an abomination!" Jado cried out, again stepping forward.

Noor lowered her head, and her tail fanned out to reveal an iridescent pattern of red and black.

Noor! Kiva warned.

The kiraeen reluctantly collapsed the end of her tail, and lowered to the floor with petulant exasperation. *I wasn't going to kill him,* she complained. *I'd only have taken a hand… an arm at most.* If she hadn't been pouting before, she most certainly was now.

Kiva ignored Jado and continued, "I understand…that there is a time and a place for tradition, but just because something was decided centuries ago, does not mean it is *right*. I stand here before you as proof of that."

"And what would you have us do?" Councilman Elam spoke up. "Our traditions are what make us who we are. Do you believe we should abandon them? Abandon our identity?"

"I would never suggest such a thing," Kiva said vehemently.

"Yet you continue to violate our laws, and break with our ways."

"Tell me, councilman, what is our greatest tradition?"

The late-aged man with graying hair furrowed his brow. Kiva stared at him, unflinching.

"I suppose...our greatest tradition would be convention...adherence to the order and laws of our society," he answered confidently.

"A good tradition," Kiva responded, "But *not* the greatest."

Councilman Elam's expression soured. "And I suppose you, a girl not yet past her adolescence, would know better than her elders?"

Kiva turned away from him to face the crowd. "Centuries ago, when our people were forced from our homeworld, was it convention that gave us the courage to leave everything behind?"

Some of those in the crowd were looking at each other with uncertainty.

"When my great grandfather, and all of those in the basin, were faced with the great drought—a threat so severe that we nearly lost everything—was it *convention* that led every last sect to re-purpose its focus on finding a solution?"

"I recall the great drought," elder councilman Daivari said thoughtfully. His voice became somber. "I was only a boy, though I still recall the cries of the dying."

"Councilman Elam," Kiva continued, "We are in agreement on one thing. Our traditions are what make us who we are—the greatest of which is the tradition of abandoning *convention* when it impedes the survival of our people."

Jado barked a laugh. "And you think allowing *female* windwalkers will '*save our people*' from some nonexistent threat?"

Kiva turned to see the windwalker sidi wearing a sardonic smile. "As you already know, Sidi Jado, the threat is hardly nonexistent."

His smile melted, and his eyes narrowed.

Kiva turned back to the crowd. "At this very moment, great sandstorms sweep across the desert to the southwest."

Another low, unsettled murmur worked its way through the crowd.

"That is not all," she continued. "Not two hours ago, I witnessed what I thought was ash falling from the sky. It was not ash, but flakes of rain-frost, and by the time I'd left, it had painted the ground in a blanket of white."

"Meddling girl!" Jado cried out, glaring at Noor.

The crowd's tone had grown to concerned conversation.

"To the northeast, blood red Garra flowers bloom in vast number upon the Mujdab Plains, where no life has taken hold for hundreds of years."

Shouts began breaking out. Kiva was hit with a sudden wave of doubt. *What am I doing confronting the council? This is madness…*

It was then that Noor's raw tenacity heated her blood. *The man you call Jado is a coward. You possess more strength than these landbound groundwalkers.*

Reinvigorated by Noor's stark appraisal, Kiva raised her voice, "For centuries, we have known peace. But any familiar with our past can tell you, it was not always so." She paused, and waited as the crowd quieted to an agitated murmur. "You know of whom I speak."

"That is *enough*," Elam shouted.

"Let her speak!" voices from the crowd responded, and the bitter councilman scowled.

"You preach of tradition," Kiva said, turning to him. "What do our traditions say of heeding the warnings of our ancestors?" She turned back to the crowd.

"*The sands rose up and named us foe, The plains wept blood where nothing would grow, Upon dunes painted white, the Sharun take flight, Reaping death and despair, in the absence of light.*"

Silence again returned, and Kiva knew she had their full attention.

"The signs are clear, yet those whose duty it is to heed them have remained silent," Kiva said, pointing back toward Jado.

"This is preposterous!" Jado shouted. "This…child has no—"

Daivari raised a palm toward him, and he quieted in disbelief. "Is it true, councilman?" Daivari asked. "Are the signs present?"

"Neither myself, nor my windwalkers have encountered any *frozen ash*. As I said, it is preposterous." He was nearly ranting.

"And the sandstorms? The blood flowers?" Daivari persisted.

Jado's expression darkened, and his silence was answer enough.

Angry shouts came from those watching, only this time they were directed at Jado.

"Peace," Daivari called out, again raising his palms to the crowd.

"The signs are clear," Kiva said, and the shouts subsided. "The Sharun will soon be upon us. We must prepare to fight, or be destroyed."

Concerned voices again rose from the crowd. People turned to each other with worried expressions.

"How many have challenged the windwalker sect in the past ten years?" Kiva asked. "At this moment, there are fewer members than there have been in the past century…and even if none will admit it, the same holds true for the other sects sworn to defend. We have grown complacent. We *must* train new warriors," Kiva said with conviction, driving a fist into her palm.

"I will fight!" a shout came from an unnamed voice in the crowd, and was echoed by others.

"And how are we to find the additional warriors?" The voice that came from behind belonged to a woman. It was Netaniah.

Kiva smiled on the inside. The weaver sidi was helping lead her to the point. Before Kiva could answer, the fourth male councilman—who had been quiet up until then—spoke, "If it is true, and the signs are present, then I will commit the builder sect to defend."

Daivari nodded to him with respect. "If this threat proves true, we will need men from all sects to stand together."

"There is no threat!" Jado screamed, his eyes bulging.

"Enough, Jado," Daivari said firmly.

The crowd became increasingly agitated.

"It will not be enough," Kiva said loudly, drawing more than a few fearful eyes.

Elam responded, still wearing a scowl, "This *girl* would suggest we give up!" he called out, seizing on the opportunity. "Abandon our homes!"

"No!" Kiva shouted. "I say we fight! All of us!" There was a brief moment of confusion, and Kiva sensed that her time was nearly up. "For each male sect sworn to defend our people, we create a female twin, dedicated to the same cause."

The crowd objected vociferously, and Elam's scowl turned into a smug smile.

"I am proof that it is possible!" Kiva insisted, but the crowd was no longer listening.

"I am sorry, Kivanya," Councilman Daivari said, gently placing a wrinkled hand on her arm. Noor raised her head, which had been resting on the stone floor. "We have strayed far from the original purpose of this trial." He turned to the others. "If the council will take their seats, we will begin the vote." The elder councilman turned and shuffled back to his bench as the others sat.

Fools. Noor's thought came to Kiva as she turned to face the council.

"Kivanya Raisel Fariq, you stand accused of violating sect enrollment protocol, trespassing on sect land, public disruption, and the death of a kiraeen belonging to the windwalker sect."

Death of a kiraeen? Kiva's eyes widened with shock. She looked to Jado, who was watching her with smug satisfaction. Kiva remembered back to the trials. Noor must have killed one of the males while defending her. Noor's unapologetic confirmation came almost immediately.

"Do you deny the charges?" Daivari asked.

Even the day before, Kiva would have denied responsibility for the kiraeen's death. But she and Noor were bonded now—their fates intertwined.

"I do not," Kiva said defiantly as a wave of feathers ruffled across Noor's back.

Daivari failed to mask his surprise, and Noor raised herself up to full height. Nataniah was frowning, looking to Kiva with furrowed brows, and Jado's smug smile had grown into a grin.

"Do you understand clearly the charges brought against you, child? The penalty?" Daivari asked, his eyes imploring her to reconsider her answer.

"What I understand," she said gravely, "is that if we fail to recognize when our long held beliefs have become obsolete, we will perish. You refuse to see what is plainly before you. I am a windwalker in all but name. You may condemn me, but in doing so you condemn us all."

The entire proceeding fell completely silent, as if every last person held their breath.

Daivari sighed, and his bushy white eyebrows drooped.

"The charges stand," Daivari's somber voice carried out over the silence. "All in favor?"

Kiva's heart pounded in her chest as the four male council members, including the elder Daivari, raised their right hands.

"Opposed?"

The four female council members raised theirs, canceling out the men.

Daivari looked to the women at his left, then right to the men. "It would seem the procedure for a tie will be tested in our very first trial of equal representation…" He stood, raising his voice, "Four votes for, and four against. The final decision falls to our eldest mystic, Sidi Yehiel." A long pause followed, and the murmur of the crowd again grew. Daivari looked around. "Where is he? Where is Yehiel?"

A young man in orange robes climbed the stairs at the edge of the stage and waited there. Daivari waved him over impatiently, and they exchanged words, too quietly for Kiva to hear. The young man quickly departed the stage, leaving Daivari with a thoughtful expression on his face.

After a moment, he spoke, "It would seem Sidi Yehiel is unable to provide the necessary ruling. In his stead, the next eldest mystic, Sufiin Suriel, will settle the matter."

A spark of hope flared to life inside Kivanya. Suriel… Yehiel's sister.

Honestly, Noor interjected, *I don't see why you would even want to remain here. If these groundwalkers don't desire our protection from the coming storm, then they do not deserve it.*

This is my home, Kiva responded. *These are my people… even if some are misguided.*

Noor communicated the kiraeen equivalent of a shrug, and settled back into a crouch.

Moments later, Kiva caught sight of the young mystic in orange robes leading a hunched figure in white through the crowd. It was Suriel, leaning on her cane with one hand, and the man's arm with the other. Slowly but surely, they made their way, and eventually arrived at the stage. As they ascended the stairs and moved toward the center of the platform, the orange robed mystic's wide eyes were on Noor the entire time. Suriel gave the kiraeen a quick glance, and that was all. As they passed Kiva, the elder tilted her head, giving Kiva a good once over. "Quite the fuss, for one so young," she said softly enough that only Kiva and the escort could hear.

The crowd quieted as the young man left Suriel on the stage and backed away, giving Noor a wide berth.

If the elder was at all intimidated, she gave no indication. To Kiva, she seemed more cranky than anything else.

"Per the newly established council rules…I, Sufiin Suriel of the sect of mystics, will decide this girl's fate, since you all can't make up your own minds," she said, craning her neck to glare at the council.

"Kivanya Fariq will *not* face exile," she said simply, and the crowd erupted in cheers loud enough to drown out any who disagreed.

Kiva felt every muscle in her body relax. *I can stay!* she rejoiced, and Noor couldn't help but brighten at her reaction.

"Shame on you," she said, shaking her cane at the council. "She is a *child*. Did you make no mistakes in your youth? Or was it so long ago that you've forgotten? And they call me old!"

Kiva frowned.

Jado was again scowling, and the other councilmen shifted uncomfortably on their benches. Nataniah wore a small, relieved smile.

For the first time, Kiva caught a glimpse of her mother standing at the rear corner of the stage. She was looking at Kiva sternly, shaking her head.

A child? Kiva thought. *Mistakes?* If she were a kiraeen, her tail would have been flicking erratically.

Perhaps before the bond, Kiva might have held her tongue and accepted the free pass she'd been given. But as it were, she was bonded to a skyhunter—a tenaciously prideful creature of immeasurable strength and majesty. That bond carried with it a fusing of personality, and Noor would *never* have tolerated being treated that way.

"Sufiin Suriel," Kiva said respectfully.

"Hmm?" The old woman turned to face her, still fully unintimidated by Noor's imposing presence. "What is it, child?"

"I am grateful for your decision—"

"A young person with little experience of the world should not be held to the same standard as a fully grown woman. Remember this as you mature. I expect to hear no more of this *windwalker* foolishness, do I make myself clear? Your mother should have known better than to raise you as such."

Kiva abandoned all pretenses of respect, and her blood began to boil. "You have no right to criticize my mother! She is a strong woman who is not afraid to fight for what she believes in."

"I see. It becomes clear to me where you acquired your lack of respect for your elders…for tradition."

"If not for her, there would be three women seated behind you, not four."

"And I would be at home sipping a hot cup of sahlab,

instead of here, speaking to an ungrateful tifl tufuliun. Perhaps I was mistaken to let you off so easily."

Kiva could almost hear her mother's voice in her head, pleading for her to give over.

"I do not *require* your approval," Kiva said venomously. "Despite what you think, I am not a child, and nothing of what I did was a mistake. *I* am fighting for the future survival of our people, while qadim like you fight tooth and nail to hold us back!"

There were several gasps from the crowd, and Kiva suddenly realized there were witnesses to the exchange. She knew what she was doing would be unforgivable, but she was sick and tired of being dismissed.

"If you will not accept what I am," Kiva declared, "if my only choice is that of false repentance, or exile…then I choose exile."

"*Kiva no!*" her mother cried out, but it was too late.

"Very well," Suriel said. "You shall have your wish." She turned to face the crowd. Those in the front were stunned to silence, but the vast majority were unaware of what was coming.

"Kivanya Raisel Fariq, you are hereby sentenced to exile. Under penalty of death, you shall never again set foot in Madina Basin. Any foolish enough to communicate with you shall join you in your banishment. You are forsaken." Without another word, Suriel turned and began shuffling her way back to the stairs, as the younger mystic in orange robes rushed over to meet her.

The blood drained from Kiva's face as the ramifications

hit home. She looked down at her hands, which were pale and shaking.

We do not need them, Noor insisted.

Kiva's hands balled into fists. She could feel the prick of burning tears, forcing their way past her crumbling defenses. Rather than give Jado and the others the satisfaction, Kiva turned, and Noor lowered herself. In seconds she was again on the kiraeen's back, and they were launched up into the sky, soaring out beyond the walls of the basin.

EXILE

Kiva's tears were wiped away by the rushing wind. She and Noor flew in silence overv the desert, drifting lazily on the failing thermals. The sun had set, and sparkling swathes of stars had begun to reveal themselves against the darkening sky.

As the rest of the world fell away, Kiva rested her tear-stained cheek against Noor's soft, black feathers. Cool air rushed past, and Kiva clung desperately to the memories of her mother, father, and brothers. Her heart ached fiercely at the prospect of losing them forever, but there was another for which the anguish was nearly unbearable.

You barely know him, she berated herself, hoping for logic to win out over emotion.

Noor remained silent, occasionally flapping her great wings as they traveled. Kiva stared aimlessly down toward the dimly lit desert floor. It was of little consequence to her that the landscape had changed from jagged rocky buttes to great unmoving waves of sand.

Somewhere in the back of her mind, it registered that Noor was taking them home. The great stone wall where they'd had their first encounter rose up out of the sand in the distance, and Noor began descending toward it. Moments later, she held her wings out and they glided into the blackness of her den.

Kiva should have been blinded by the utter darkness, but through Noor's sight, she could sense the faint outlines of the cavern. The kiraeen set down within, and lowered herself. Kiva slid over her side. The strain of her loss was too great, and her legs collapsed. Noor caught Kiva gently with her wing, and lowered her to the soft down surface of her nest.

Kiva drifted in the black, cradled between Noor's wing and her soft body. It was only the anchor of Noor's presence and warmth that kept Kiva from drifting forever in a sea of hopelessness.

Eventually, even the feathers faded as Kiva relinquished her grasp on consciousness, drifting into an uneasy, dreamless sleep.

***

"Kivanya!"

Kiva blinked, still trapped within the hazy limbo between waking and sleep.

"Kiva…you there?"

Noor's head rested on the cavern floor, though she was awake, and keenly aware of the presence near the mouth of her den.

Kiva squinted, peering toward the blindingly bright cavern opening. As her eyes adjusted, a dark silhouette came into focus.

"Jonah?" Kiva pushed herself up, unsure whether to trust her senses.

"Kiva!" he called, climbing up onto the uneven floor of the cavern.

She stumbled to her feet and half-staggered, half-ran toward him. They collided in an explosive, ardent embrace. Kiva gripped him tightly, pressing her face against his chest. He held her just as tightly, and for a brief moment, they were no longer pupil and teacher. They were Kivanya and Jonah, two windwalkers who had found something more powerful even than the bond of a kiraeen.

They parted, and Kiva realized her cheeks were damp.

As relieved as she was to see him, she thought him foolish to come.

"You can't be here," she said. "If anyone were to find out, you'd be exiled—"

"No one knows where I am," he assured her.

She turned away from him, ashamed at having failed. "I thought I'd never see you again." Ever since their first meeting, Kiva had done her best to ignore the powerful feelings he evoked in her. Given everything she'd been through, denying how she felt about him seemed small and pointless.

"Hey," he said, gently turning her chin forward. "This isn't over."

"Didn't you hear?" Kiva asked, "I've been *exiled*. I can *never* go home again. I've failed."

"Jado has been removed from the council," Jonah said bluntly.

"He what?"

"Once word got out that he was hiding signs of the Sharun's return, he lost his seat on the council. Nothing else has been decided as of yet, but there's a good chance he'll lose leadership of the windwalkers as well."

Kiva was stunned to silence.

Jonah smiled. "You did well, Kivanya Fariq. Preparations have begun. The sects are banding together to withstand what comes."

Kiva felt a weight off her shoulders that she hadn't realized she'd been carrying. Whether or not she was there to help, her people would now have a better chance for survival.

"Now all that's left is to convince them to lift your exile," he said, as if it were a simple household chore.

"They don't *want* me," she argued.

"Most do…and besides, it doesn't much matter what they want. Right now, they *need* you. There's something special inside you, Kiva. I knew it from the moment I first saw you. If we are going to survive the coming storm, we are going to need your strength. *I* am going to need you."

Kiva felt a wave of warmth pass from the top of her scalp, down to the tips of her toes. Without thinking, she stepped forward into his arms, and pressed her lips to his. Her heart raced in her chest, the tiny hairs on the back of her neck stood on end, and goosebumps covered her arms. It was nearly perfect…but something was off.

Kiva stepped back, nervously biting her lip.

Jonah's expression was uncertain.

"I…sorry," Kiva said looking away. "I thought—"

"No," he said. "It's my fault…I…" He stammered, running a hand through his hair.

"You don't have to explain," Kiva pursed her lips. She

grasped for something to change the subject…anything. "The female combat sects," she said, "Is there any word on whether the idea took hold?"

Jonah shook his head, clearly grateful for the diversion. "Not outright, but there is talk of it. You've quite the knack for controversy," he said with a small smile.

Kiva smiled back, but on the inside she was still cursing herself for her brashness.

Kiva sensed Noor rising. *I could remove his head,* she interjected. *Would that please you?*

What? Kiva thought, aghast. *Absolutely not! What is wrong with you?*

Suit yourself, Noor thought, settling back down into her nest.

Jonah continued, unaware of the exchange, "I should probably get going. The windwalker and shadestalker sects are mounting an attack."

Kiva's eyes widened. "Already? How?"

Jonah nodded. "The council ordered verification of the Garra bloom on the Mujdab plains. Once we arrived there, we found more than just flowers. Twisted black stone spires had grown up from the rock. We think they are connected to how the Sharun travel here."

Kiva furrowed her brow.

"But the plains are far to the northeast, and the sandstorms have been strongest here in the southwest…it was here I witnessed the frozen ash," Kiva insisted.

"Once we've toppled the spires, we will begin searching for shade signs out this way. The last time our people faced the Sharun, the struggle lasted for decades. If we can stop them early this time—prevent them from growing in number—maybe we can end the attack before it begins. The council has asked me to lead the windwalker attack, while they decide what to do with Jado. This time, we bring the fight to them."

"I can help," Kiva said. "There could be resistance." Kiva recalled the fables of the long dead heroes who fought the towering Sharun shades rising up from the sand and shadows.

"Not this time," Jonah said. "If Jado is removed as windwalker sidi, then the council may be willing to dismiss the charges he brought against you. That might not happen if you suddenly appear alongside the attack party."

Kiva sighed.

"We will beat this, Kivanya," he said, placing a hand on her shoulder. "I promise. One way or another, you *will* bear the title of windwalker."

"I hate sitting around waiting. I want to fight."

"And you will. Just not today," Jonah said, glancing back. "I have to go, but I will return with news after the attack." He turned and walked back toward the den's entrance.

"Jonah," Kiva called, and he turned back. "Good hunting."

He smiled, turned, and leapt out from the cavern opening. Seconds later, he and Zakai swooped back up, climbing high on the thermals.

I don't understand, Noor thought.

"What?" Kiva asked aloud.

Why you tolerate the males of your species.

"I wonder that myself, at times," Kiva admitted. "Come

on, I'm starving. Let's find something to eat."

Noor climbed forward out of her nest, and Kiva pulled herself onto the skyhunter's back. She had discarded the bonding harness, which was no longer necessary. Instead of pushing or pulling on straps, Kiva only had to think, and Noor obliged. They soared out into the sunshine. Being more familiar with the landscape, Noor choose their path. Kiva looked down at their shadow, speeding up and down the sand dunes below. After several minutes of drifting, Noor began to descend toward a small oasis, spotted with trees and sparse grass.

It was there she deposited Kiva, before lifting off again to hunt. Kiva walked up to the calm pool of water and filled her skins. She drank deep, and washed her face. A spring such as this was exceedingly rare in the Miralaja. Finding them was another benefit of flight.

Once refreshed, Kiva set about gathering brush from nearby scraggly shrubs, and sticks from the occasional stunted and gnarled tree. She was in the process of building a fire when she felt a primal surge of satisfaction. Somewhere to the east, Noor had caught her prey.

Soon Kiva could see, as well as sense the kiraeen soaring toward her, something large dangling from her rear talons. Noor descended, landing nearby. Locked into her razor sharp claws was an enormous snake, easily twice as long as Kiva was tall.

Noor chirped, and Kiva nodded respectfully.

The head is mine, Noor thought, before tearing the rear third of the snake off and tossing it toward Kiva. Not one to turn her nose up at a free meal, Kiva went to work removing the skin and stripping the meat from the bones. Soon the crackling fire was host to multiple strips of meat, which Kiva cooked on long sticks.

Meanwhile, Noor tore at the snake's head, picking out the eyes with her sharp beak. Once they'd both had their fill, Kiva stood and looked northeast, toward the Mujdab Plains. Jonah likely wouldn't be returning until nightfall.

I don't know about you, Kiva thought, *But I don't plan on sitting around doing nothing while we wait for him to come back.*

Let us hunt the Sharun, Noor thought with anticipation.

We can't. Not yet. Kiva frowned. *But we can scout the desert to the south.*

A wave of ruffled feathers ran over Noor's body.

What? Kiva asked.

That way is cursed.

Cursed? What do you mean?

The wind bites, the ground bears no prey, and blood pours from the land.

Kiva paused, considering. *I think then, that is exactly where we must go.*

Noor flicked her tail in agitation, but understood that Kiva saw a connection between that place and the Sharun—ancient enemy of both Sahra' and kiraeen.

Fine, Noor agreed, and they once again lifted off, leaving the oasis behind.

They soared southward, farther than Kiva had ever traveled. She soon began to understand Noor's misgivings. The air temperature was dropping steadily. Kiva wrapped her head tightly in her black scarf, and fished her goggles out from a small pouch at her waist.

Down below, the waves of desert sand appeared to have broken upon red stone hardpan, riddled with cracks and debris. Swirling funnels of wind threw red dust into the air, creating an ominous reddish-brown haze.

Satisfied? Noor asked, hoping Kiva would turn back.

Not yet.

Noor pumped her wings, driving them forward. Down below, Kiva spotted clumps of blood-red garra flowers through the occasional gaps in the haze. *They must grow more easily at colder temperatures,* she thought. Her eyes were drawn by a sudden great gust of wind, approaching from her left. Noor changed course to meet it head on, and was able to hover in place without beating her wings as the cool air rushed under them.

Kiva ducked her head, pressing her body flat against Noor's. Once the gust had blown past, Noor tipped her wings, turning them southward, and Kiva looked down at the ground in disbelief. The wind had carried away the obfuscating haze of red dust, revealing a cracked and broken landscape. The garra flowers growing near the openings in the ground did indeed look like blood pouring from a wound. Among them, stretching off into the distance in great, immeasurable number, were twisted, black spires of the Sharun.

Distant thunder rumbled across the sky, punctuating the growing dread in her heart.

Those were not here last I came to this cursed place, Noor thought upon feeling Kiva's distress.

Tall, dark thunderheads began rapidly coalescing off toward the southern horizon, and another gust of icy wind blew past. Small flashes of lightning lit the foreboding clouds, and Kiva realized they were growing larger.

They're moving this way, Kiva thought with alarm.

I suggest we turn back, Noor responded, but Kiva could only stare at the swirling mass of darkness, gaining in size and strength.

She furrowed her brow. "Those aren't storm clouds," she said with rising fear. "Khamsim," she whispered under her breath. "Sandstorm!"

It rushed toward them at a speed that should have been impossible for something so large.

Noor abruptly changed course, instinctively bolting for the safety of her den.

No! Kiva thought desperately, *We have to warn the basin!*

You mean those cowards who sentenced you to exile?

They're not all bad, she admitted. *My family...*

Kiva could sense Noor's displeasure, yet she begrudgingly altered their heading, toward the basin. The kiraeen's wings pumped mechanically, and Kiva's braids trailed behind her as they sped high over the cracked and broken desert floor.

"There," Kiva said, pointing to a nearby thermal. The thick column of wavy, semi-transparent air climbed skyward. Noor adjusted the angle of her rear pinions and they hit it moments later, climbing as they flew.

A glance back revealed the massive storm, towering up to unimaginable heights. It had gotten much closer, or much larger. Either option was bad. It was normally an hour's flight to the basin, but if they continued at this speed they'd reach it in half the time—perhaps with enough of a head start to raise the alarm.

Kiva held her body close to Noor's in order to maintain as low a profile as possible. After another few minutes, she looked back and found they had put some distance between themselves and the storm-front.

We're doing it! Kiva thought. *The storm is falling behind.*

And once we're there? Noor asked. *The basin walls will not keep this storm out.*

Kiva didn't answer. The ancient sandshields lining the tops of the basin walls hadn't been raised in her lifetime, or her parents', for that matter. They'd never had the need. The largest storm Kiva had seen was easily dwarfed by the basin walls. *This* was something else entirely. Storms like this one were the reason they built the sandshields in the first place; back in the *darktime*, when Sharun attacks were commonplace.

Quickly, Kiva urged, and Noor pressed on.

Soon the walls of Madina Basin came into view; small at first, yet growing larger as they approached. No kiraeen flew over the basin, where they might have seen the storm and given warning. They were all on the hunt to the northeast.

We had no idea how far along the Sharun had come. Al'ama! We should have been ready! Kiva cursed Jado a thousand times as they descended into the basin. Noor spread her wings, slowing their speed and spiraling down around the inside walls.

Kiva sat up and cupped her hands around her mouth.

"Khamsim!" she shouted with all her strength. "Khamsim! A sandstorm approaches! Raise the sandshields!" she shouted, attempting to raise the alarm. "Khamsim!"

At first those Sahra' going about their day looked up in confusion. Sandstorms had never been a threat to them inside the basin. *Khamsim* were the storms of legend, not something they would ever have to worry about.

As Noor descended closer to the basin floor, mothers were corralling their children into their rocky abodes.

Hiding won't be enough to save them, Noor thought.

I know! Let me think!

The council could force action, but there was no time to convince them, wherever they were.

The bell! Kiva pointed to a great concave niche in the western wall. Within it hung a massive iron bell that had not been rung in a hundred years. Kiva had considered climbing to it many times, but never had the chance. Now she would not need to climb at all.

Noor beat her wings, carrying them up to the stony indentation. She perched on the opening, and Kiva slipped off her, onto the narrow surface. Before her was the bell, nearly twice as tall as she was. Kiva placed her hands on the cool iron, and pushed. The bell swung a few inches, and Kiva used it to build momentum. The clapper hit the inside of the bell, sending powerful vibrations through it. Soon it was ringing at full, deafening volume. Kiva leapt back onto Noor, who dropped from the edge back down into the basin.

I think you have their attention, Noor said as the bell clanged and clonged behind them.

"Khamsim! Sandstorm!" Kiva continued shouting. "Raise the sandshields!"

Now everyone in the basin was scrambling, rushing this way and that. The great steel shields near the top of the basin remained unmoving.

Kiva cursed, instructing Noor to fly up to the square stone opening near the base of one shield on the western wall. The shields themselves were hundreds of feet tall, ending where the tops of the basin walls did. The openings below them were large enough for the kiraeen to fit inside—all the better for windwalkers to operate them. They landed in the opening, and Kiva slid over Noor's side, running to the tall, rusted iron wheel connected to the far wall. She leapt onto it, hanging from one side and yanking downward.

"It wont budge!" she cried out in frustration.

Let me try.

Noor came forward, gripping the wall above it with the front talons atop her wings, and stepping with one of her rear talons into a spoke of the wheel. The metal squealed loudly as the wheel came loose, and Noor leapt back.

Thank you, Kiva thought as she rushed forward and wrenched the wheel around. Behind the wall came the sounds of great counterweights shifting. These were followed by the scraping of the massive, curved shield, rising up past the top of the western wall.

The sandshield *clunked* into place, casting a tall shadow into the basin. Kiva immediately leapt back onto Noor, and they swept out from the shield's control room, and onto the next. There were twelve shields all together, lining the southwestern walls. There was no way they could get them all, but Kiva was determined to try.

The second wheel came loose without her kiraeen's help, and Kiva spun it as quickly as she could before leaping back onto Noor. This time when they launched out of the opening, Kiva could see two of the other shields slowly rising up from their cradles, extending the height of the walls by hundreds of feet. Someone below had heeded her warning.

They wheeled around to the next one, but as they did, the sky went ominously dark. Kiva looked up from Noor's back to see that the sun had become a blood red circle, obscured by the vanguard of the towering sandstorm. The persistent sound of rushing sand and howling wind began to fill the basin, growing louder by the second.

Upon dunes painted white, the Sharun take flight,
Reaping death and despair, in the absence of light.

Noor's thought was ominous and cold, *It's here.*

The Storm

Quickly! The next shield! Kiva urged. Noor lunged out with Kiva clinging to her back. Her headscarf was blown back as they sped into the next shield's opening. Kiva tugged on the wheel, but it wouldn't budge. Noor leapt forward as she had before, and pried it loose, allowing Kiva to finish the job.

The wind had grown to a cacophonous howling, punctuated by deafening bouts of thunder.

One more, Kiva thought desperately. *We have to raise another!*

Noor didn't move. The opening out to the basin was filled with whipping wind and swirling sand.

A deep *boom* resonated through the basin, shaking the stone beneath Kiva's feet as the bulk of the storm crashed into the walls.

The sun was now completely blotted out, casting the basin into darkness. The occasional flash of lightning lit the roiling sand clouds above, like the glowing heartbeat of a colossal, malignant shade. Kiva pulled her headscarf tight, covering her nose, mouth and hair as the storm churned, pelting her entire body with stinging sand. The wind was deafening, blowing into the control room with such force that Kiva felt her feet sliding across the stone. She hooked an arm around the wheel and held tight.

Even with goggles on, it was impossible to see. She knew Noor was nearby, but that was all. Both of them were crouched down, heads covered, for what felt like hours as the storm relentlessly battered Madina Basin. Kiva could only hope her forewarning had been enough to save some of the lives below.

For several long minutes, the winds continued to howl and the sand flew. Kiva began to wonder if it were possible that the storm had paused its advance over the basin, remaining there indefinitely, when finally the winds began to die down.

Cautiously removing her arm from over her head, she looked out to verify what she'd hoped to be true—the storm had passed.

Kiva slowly stood, and the sand that had accumulated on her head, shoulders, and back fell to the floor. Noor stood nearby, ruffling her feathers in an attempt to rid herself of the pervasive grains of sand. Outside, the red tinged sunlight slowly transitioned to orange, then back to the bright yellow of an average afternoon.

Kiva strode across the floor—which was covered in a few inches of sand—to the large square opening of the sandshield control room. Sand covered nearly everything below. It had piled up in great drifts against the far walls, blocking the entrances to more than a few abodes. Merchant carts had been smashed, broken and battered, the goods they once contained strewn haphazardly across the basin.

No bodies, Kiva thought with relief.

None unburied by sands, Noor observed.

Not helpful, Kiva glared at the great kiraeen perched beside her.

Down below, men and women tentatively opened the boards covering their homes and peered out with wide eyes. The basin was in disarray. It would take weeks to remove all the sand. Many of the merchants will have lost their livelihood.

If not for you, they would have lost their lives as well, Noor thought, preening her sandy feathers.

Kiva was developing a growing appreciation for Noor's straightforward nature. The kiraeen would never feel sorry for her, or allow her to feel sorry for herself, for that matter. Noor was a warrior from birth to death, and she would expect nothing less from Kiva.

Someone below was struggling to get their door open. "We should go down and—"

The alarm came from Noor like a bolt of lightning, and Kiva ducked. Noor's long neck swept over her head. The kiraeen's beak snapped shut with a *clack,* and Kiva was showered in more sand. Kiva spun, curving khanjar dagger in hand.

She watched in disbelief as tendrils of sand swirled up from the floor of the control room. They coalesced, then settled into the shape of an armored warrior. In its left hand was a large round shield. In its right, a tall spear with a long spike at one end. It wore a mask shaped like the face of a wild dog, framed by two horns, curving down along the jawline. Two shadowy sockets stared out from where its eyes should have been. Within each was a crystal, darker than night and pulsing with unsettling awareness.

Sharun. Kiva and Noor shared the thought simultaneously.

Noor lowered her body, preparing to strike, but Kiva moved first. Leaping forward, she extended her leg and made contact with the sharun's shield. It staggered back, then regained its balance and stabbed at her with its spear. Kiva turned sideways, narrowly avoiding the long spike. She struck back, but the sharun was fast. It brought its shield up in time to block the attack, then again stabbed its spear toward her. Kiva evaded in the other direction, rolling to the outside of its spear arm. The advantageous position hadn't come without cost. The sharpened spike split the skin on her shoulder. Kiva ignored the pain and slashed with her dagger as she rotated her body. The blade made contact, severing the sharun's spear arm. Both arm and spear fell to the floor, disintegrating back into sand on impact.

The sharun slammed its shield into Kiva, knocking her back. Sand was traveling up along its legs and torso.

It's regenerating, Noor pointed out.

I can see that!

Kiva grit her teeth and launched another attack. She feinted high, then swiped low. Her curved dagger hooked below the shield, severing one of the sharun's feet off at the ankle. It lost its balance, falling onto its back. Kiva leapt on top of it, stabbing downward. Her blade sank into its chest, but the cold-eyed creature gave no reaction.

The arm! Noor warned.

A stump with a long spike on the end stabbed at her. Kiva rolled off, avoiding it, and quickly got to her feet. The sharun's foot was regenerating, and it was attempting to rise.

"No you don't!" she growled. Kiva planted a kick to the back of its head, sending it forward onto its face. She leapt onto its back, wrapped one arm around the head, and drew her blade across its neck.

Kiva fell back, holding the head, which disintegrated in her arms. The body did the same, and all that remained were two shadowy, swirling crystals where its eyes had been. Sand began to swirl into the air around them.

Crush them! Noor commanded.

Kiva raised her dagger with both hands and brought the pommel crashing into one of the crystals, shattering it. She quickly did the same to the other, and the floating grains fell lifelessly to the floor.

More rise…below, Noor thought, peering out of the opening. Kiva rushed over and joined her. A man was fighting one of the same sand creatures with nothing more than a block of wood. A scream pierced the air as someone else took a spear through to the shoulder.

There must be at least fifty of them, Kiva worried.

She leapt onto Noor's back and they dropped from the high ledge of the sandshield control room.

There, Kiva directed Noor toward a man desperately fighting for his life. As they grew close, Kiva shifted her weight back, and Noor tilted her own body. She spread her wings and crashed into the sharun with her rear talons, then leveled out and began climbing. The sharun exploded into a cloud of sand.

"Destroy the eyes!" Kiva shouted as they swooped back up. "They will return if you don't destroy the eyes!"

Where are the safekeepers? Kiva thought in frustration. The sect dedicated to protecting the basin had many capable warriors, but they were nowhere in sight. She directed Noor toward their sect stronghold, and found the entrance buried in sand and debris.

We have to clear it away.

Noor quickly descended to the blocked entrance, and Kiva dismounted. Together they pushed away the sand, stone, and pieces of broken carts, until half the door was visible.

Noor screeched, and Kiva turned to see another sharun stabbing toward her kiraeen. Noor wrapped her long tail around the spear and yanked it free. In a fury, the skyhunter snapped its shield away, then completely flattened the sharun with one of her powerful legs. Sand exploded into the air. Kiva quickly found the eyes and crushed them.

They could now hear yells from behind the door, and the sound of fists pounding against it. Soon they had the sand cleared away and were able to force open the door.

"Quickly!" Kiva yelled as a group of about twenty men dressed for battle poured out. They wore thick layered aga skin across their chests, and each held a small buckler shield and a short, arm's length spear with a sharpened blade at the end.

"Kivanya?" one of them asked, shocked at the sight of her.

"The exile!" proclaimed another.

Kiva's expression darkened. "Destroy the eyes," she instructed, pointing to the chaos behind her. "It's the only way to stop them."

A woman screamed across the basin, and the safekeepers

rushed out into the fray, their surprise superseded by the need to protect.

Kivanya, Noor thought, drawing her attention to the center of the basin. Hundreds, possibly thousands of sandy tendrils were swirling up from the ground. They twisted and coalesced, forming a solid body. The base of the emerging sandshade was twenty paces in diameter. It climbed at least forty paces high, growing taller still.

Kiva leapt onto Noor's back, and they sprung high into the air. Noor circled the height of the sandshade as it took the shape of an enormous, winding column, covered in downward slanting spikes. The head of the great serpent elongated, and fangs as tall as Kivanya grew down from the top and up from the bottom of its spiked, serrated maw. The sandshade had no eyes, but instead housed two large clusters of black crystals on either side of its head.

Now that it was fully formed, Kivanya and Noor were dwarfed by comparison. They were like a small clayfowl, haranguing a gigantic aga lizard.

A great hiss came from between its jaws. Down below, a safekeeper turned to face the beast. As he craned his head back to take in the sight, the whites of his eyes shone in disbelief, and his jaw hung slack. The sandshade struck. The warrior could only raise his arms up defensively as the massive jaws clamped down on his midsection. He was lifted high into the air, and the great snake pointed its nose to the sky. It opened its jaws wide, and guzzled him down into its writhing throat.

We have to stop it, Kiva thought, and Noor agreed

wholeheartedly. To the kiraeen, this was an abomination; the same ancient enemy that had forced them from their old world.

Kiva opted for Noor to lead their attack. The kiraeen climbed high above the snake, took aim, and dove. They streaked toward the great head at breakneck speed. As they grew close, Noor extended her talons and clawed at the cluster of black glass on the right side of its face. Several of the gems went flying. Noor beat her wings, diving away. The massive snake snapped after their retreat. Noor cursed as the great maw clamped down on some of her tail feathers, pulling them free.

Kiva looked back and saw a great clump of sand slough off the snake.

It's working, she thought.

Of course it is, Noor remarked, climbing high for a second attack.

Kiva was focusing on their next strike when the high pitched screams of young children drew her attention. She sat up on Noor's back and turned toward the sound. Three figures stood cornered against the wall of the basin. The larger of the three was hunched over, swinging a cane defensively. They were fully surrounded by sharun soldiers, slowly closing in.

With the keenness of her bond-enhanced eyesight, Kiva recognized the hunched figure as the cranky old qadim who had declared her exile.

Suriel.

Kiva turned, facing forward. Noor was climbing quickly,

curving around toward the rear of the great serpent's head.

Keep the sandshade busy, Kiva instructed.

What will you do?

Instead of answering, Kiva drew her dagger and leapt from Noor's back. She gauged the wind, and angled her body toward the monster. Gripping her dagger with both hands, she plunged it into the sandshade's back. Gravity and momentum drew her down, and her blade opened a long gash along it as she fell. Looking up as she descended, Kiva saw the serpent's long head swing around toward her. At that moment, Noor landed another attack, clawing at the cluster of black gems in its face. The sandshade forgot Kiva, snapping angrily toward Noor, whose agility kept her from its fangs.

Kiva hit the ground and rolled backwards, maintaining the grip on her dagger. She stood and turned, then ran toward Suriel and the children. The sharun cornering them were focused on their prey. Kiva targeted the closest one and marked it for death. She snuck up behind and wrapped an arm around its head, then pulled her curved dagger through its neck. The head, which had been wearing the mask of an eagle, disintegrated in her arms. She stomped on its crystal eyes before tearing through the next. She'd eliminated three of the ten before they realized what was happening.

Once she had their attention, Kiva backed off in an attempt to draw them away.

"Kivanya?" Suriel's husky voice was thick with disbelief.

"Run!" Kiva shouted as the remaining sharun began advancing on her.

Suriel gathered the children, and the three of them hurried for the safety of a nearby abode.

Kiva glanced behind her and found four more sharun that had given up on attacking closed doors to come for her. Another two swirled up from the sand, closing off her only escape.

I'm trapped! Kiva thought in a panic.

Noor immediately gave up harrying the serpent to assist.

Even with the kiraeen's help, there were too many to fight without being skewered. Kiva realized with growing dread the only option available to her. She had no choice but to attempt the harab maneuver. Taking a defensive stance, she projected her intent to Noor. The kiraeen understood immediately, pulling her wings in and diving toward Kiva.

The sharun warriors edged cautiously closer, and one thrust a stabbing spear toward her midsection. Kiva parried the attack with her dagger.

Hurry!

Noor's screech came from behind, and Kiva watched as the air currents preceding Noor's dive swirled around her. She instinctively thrust her arms outward, and less than a second later they were gripped in Noor's talons. Kiva lifted her legs, avoiding the spears of the surrounding sharun, and they soared up to safety.

We did it! Kiva thought with heart-pounding relief.

Noor climbed high, skirting the walls of the basin, and keeping her distance from the serpent. It was much thinner than it had been thanks to Noor, but the great beast was still a force to be reckoned with. It smashed its head into a closed door, splintering the wood to bits. Two sharun entered the abode soon after.

Noor kept climbing up over the basin. Once they had adequate height, the kiraeen opened her talons. Kiva dropped, controlling her fall and watching below. Seconds later, Noor was there. Kiva landed on her back, gripping feathers with one hand, and holding her dagger out behind with the other.

It was just as Jonah had said. They flew not as kiraeen and rider, but as a single, indissoluble unit.

As if summoned from memory, Kiva spied three dark shapes speeding through the sky far to the east. *Windwalkers,* Kiva thought. *But so few?* She realized then she'd been so worried about the basin, she hadn't thought of what might happen if Jonah and the others were caught in the massive storm without shelter.

You better not have gotten yourself killed, she thought.

Noor angled for another strike at the sandshade serpent, and Kiva prepared herself. They swooped down, again angling for the cluster of black gems on its face. As they drew near, the serpent anticipated their attack, and Noor was forced to break off. They avoided its snapping jaws, and had begun to swoop back up when Kiva felt something wrap around her ankle.

Before she realized what had happened, she was yanked from Noor's back. She swung down, dangling by her ankle from the sandshade's long, rough tongue. It drew her in toward its enormous fangs. Kiva curled her body up, gripped the tongue, and severed it with several slashes of her dagger.

With nothing to hold her up, Kiva fell backwards toward the ground. Unable to reach her in time, Noor screeched in despair.

Kiva hit the sand hard, and the wind was knocked from her lungs. She gasped desperately for air as her vision acquired a dark vignette around the edges. Time began slipping, and she could no longer tell whether what she saw was real, or a dream. More kiraeen swooped down, attacking the serpent. Great chunks of sand sloughed off it. Suddenly, a single, riderless kiraeen—larger than the others—streaked through the air across her vision. It collided with the serpent's neck, bursting through the other side. The sandshade's head was divided from its body. It toppled, tumbling down end over end. Kiva's consciousness faded before it hit the ground.

Protection

Kiva slowly opened her eyes to a dark room. Her ribs ached, and her head was throbbing painfully with every beat of her heart. She groaned, and a blurred figure appeared, leaning over her.

"Jonah?" she mumbled.

There was a brief pause before an answer came, "No little moon. It's Papa."

"Papa," she repeated, lost in a haze of confusing shadows. "Am I dead?"

"Far from it," he answered.

Welcome back.

Kiva furrowed her brows. The thought was not her own. *How…*

Her memories began to return.

Noor?

Kiva attempted to rise, and was rewarded for her efforts with a stab of pain in her side.

Her father placed a hand on her shoulder. "You need to rest, Kivanya. You took quite the fall."

"The basin!" Kiva said with sudden urgency as memories of the attack returned.

"The threat has passed," he said calmly. "You are safe." He moved his hand to Kiva's forehead, gently pressing her head back onto the pillow.

"What about Mama? Mica? Amir?"

"All fine," he said.

"*Al'ama!*" an old woman's voice came from the doorway. "Why did you not tell me she awoke?"

"She only just—"

"*Pah!*" the unfamiliar woman muttered, elbowing him aside.

Kiva still couldn't focus well enough to discern her features.

A healer. Her groggy mind was able to grasp at least that much.

The woman moved quickly. She reached down, then smeared something across Kiva's forehead. The pungency was overwhelming, and Kiva's eyelids became too heavy to hold open.

***

"Please! I must see her!"

Kiva stirred at the plea. She was unsure how much time had passed since she last woke, but there was light streaming through the circular window in the stone wall, and the throbbing in her head had receded.

"She is not ready for visitors," her father said sternly.

Kiva strained to hear the conversation taking place in the hall outside her room.

"I swear, I'll not disturb her. I just need to see her."

I know that voice, Kiva thought.

"Jonah?" she called weakly.

"Kiva!" he shouted.

"Oh just let him in already," her mother said in exasperation.

Seconds later, Jonah stood in the doorway of her room.

His hair was even more disheveled than usual, and he looked as if he hadn't slept in days.

"Kiva," he said, rushing over and kneeling where she lay.

She felt the warmth of his hand on hers.

"I am so sorry," he said, his eyes pained.

"Not your fault," Kiva breathed.

"I should have been here," he sighed.

Kiva squeezed his hand. "Turned out alright."

Jonah met her gaze, his dark shaggy hair spilling across his forehead. "Because of you," he said. "If you hadn't given warning, and raised the sandshields…there would be far fewer of us left."

"It wasn't enough," she said, recalling those who had fallen by the sharun's hand.

"The entire basin sings your praise, Kiva. You are a hero."

Kiva was stunned into silence. She hadn't considered her actions heroic; she had only done what she could in the moment, what she assumed anyone in her position would have tried to do. Even Noor, who had never once given praise, was emanating pride at sharing a bond with one as strong willed and determined as she.

Jonah's eyes swept over her bandaged body. "Never again,"

he said. "I'll never let anything like this happen to you again. I swear it, on my bond."

Kiva frowned. "Jonah Basara," she said sternly. He was looking at her with such genuine concern and worry that her own expression softened. "I appreciate the sentiment, but you must allow *me* to take responsibility for my choices. I am a *windwalker*, not a child to be kept in your care."

"But I..." he trailed off, looking away. Jonah was clearly distraught.

"Look," she said. "If you insist on *protecting* me, then you must accept the same from me in equal measure."

When he turned to face her again, there were tears welling in his eyes. "I thought I'd lost you," he whispered.

Kiva breathed a small smile as she realized it was not concern and worry that drove him to say such things. It was love. Unmistakable, profound, enduring, all consuming love.

Kiva placed her free hand to the side of his head. Ignoring the pain in her chest, she drew his lips to hers. The same electrifying thrill coursed through her body, sending tingles through her skin. The way he kissed her back left no doubt in her mind he felt the same.

"*Ahem*," her father cleared his throat, and Jonah nearly fell over trying to scoot back.

"Ustaaz Fariq! I was just...we were just—" Jonah stammered.

"I *know* what you were doing," he said, his brows knitting together in displeasure.

"Papa, *I* kissed *him*," Kiva insisted.

"That's not how it appeared to me," he answered, glaring at Jonah.

Kiva's mother appeared behind him, smiling. "Oh come now Haruk," she said, trying to steer him out of the room.

Kiva's father sighed loudly, glaring at Jonah. "Out."

"Yes Ustaaz. Thank you," Jonah stood and bowed his head hastily. He took three steps, then turned to Kiva. "I'll see you at the celebration," he said with a grin, then turned and sidestepped around her father.

"Celebration? What celebration?" she asked, but he was already out the door. "Mama, Papa? What celebration?"

"In good time," her mother answered. "First, you need to eat something."

EXULTATION

The following day, sounds of celebration rang throughout the basin. Kiva sat up, albeit slowly, in anticipation. Her parents had been infuriatingly sparse with details about what was happening. Whatever it was, it had, by the sound of things, filled the basin floor with crowds at least as large as those for the proving ceremonies.

"You're sure you're up for it?" her father asked. The great barrel chested man stood before her with his arms crossed.

"I'm fine Papa…really!" Kiva answered. There was no *way* she was missing it. The idea of being cooped up for even another *day* made her want to run screaming.

"Alright," he answered, still not sounding fully convinced. He turned to leave, and a moment later, her mother came in to help her get ready.

Kiva slowly rose to her feet with her mother's help. There was a constant discomfort in her chest, but the sharp pains were far less frequent.

"You will see this Jonah today?" her mother asked.

Kiva flushed, and her mother smiled.

They walked over to a small wooden bench, and Kiva sat down.

"The boy is very brave…" her mother said as she brushed Kiva's long black hair.

Kiva recalled the fuzzy memory of four kiraeen, striking at the sandshade serpent before she lost consciousness. Jonah had been among them.

"...Approaching your father and I for help, when you were stuck atop the walls?" her mother finished.

It was not the reason for bravery Kiva had expected.

"When he told Papa you were injured, and that it was his *fault*..."

"It *wasn't* his fault," Kiva insisted.

"Do you honestly think it would have made a difference to Papa? He nearly marched straight to the council to put a stop to your training."

"You prevented him?" Kiva asked.

"It would have been disastrous for our cause. He had no choice but to wait, and trust that you would take care of yourself. And as for Jonah..."

Kiva could hear the smile on her mother's lips.

"He's just lucky he had nothing to do with your latest injuries..."

Kiva rolled her eyes. Her Papa could be so protective, but she loved him anyway.

"I have seen the way that boy looks at you," her mother said. "You know your father and I weren't much older than you two when we wed."

There was a long pause. *Marriage?* The idea seemed scarier than a pack of sharun warriors. "Windwalkers can't marry, Mama."

"Is that what *he* says?" her mother asked. "If that sharmoot means to lie with you without—"

"Mama!" Kiva turned to her mother, aghast. "It's not *'what he says,'* it is just how things have always been."

"I see, and because things have always been so, they should remain as such?"

Kiva had no response. In truth she wasn't sure whether *she* ever wanted to marry. What would Noor think of such an arrangement?

Just then, Kiva felt Noor ruffle her feathers at the thought.

"Just be careful, that's all I'm saying," her mother continued gently. "You know how to fly, how to fight…but love is something else entirely." She stepped around before Kiva and cupped her face with her hands. "I am *so* proud of you Kivanya."

Kiva smiled back at her beautiful mother. "And I am proud of you, Mama. We did it. After all this time, the council has balance."

Kiva's mother released her face and wrapped her arms around her.

Kiva yelped at the sharp pain in her side, and her mother released her immediately.

"Sorry!"

"It's fine," Kiva said, forcing a smile.

They spent the next half hour getting her dressed, as the celebrations continued out in the basin. Once ready, they walked from her room into the social room of their abode. Mica and Amir were there, sitting on pillows playing stones. They both stood at her arrival.

"Kiva!" Mica said, grinning broadly. "You look awful!"

Tsk. Her mother scolded.

Kiva turned to her, "We keeping pet goats in the house now? Why does this one speak to me?"

Mica laughed, walking forward to hug her.

"Careful!" her mother warned.

Mica settled for placing his hands on her shoulders. "I am glad you're okay, little sister," he said genuinely.

"And you, brother," she said smiling.

Amir stepped up behind him, and Mica moved aside.

He was looking away, and she could tell he was wrestling with something difficult. After an awkward pause, Kiva was preparing to speak when he blurted out, "I doubted you."

Kiva watched, waiting for him to continue.

He looked at the floor as he spoke, "I thought you were being a rude, mule-headed, disrespectful, selfish, ungrateful—"

"I *think* I get the idea," Kiva said, raising an eyebrow.

He looked up into her eyes, and she saw something there that she'd never expected. Amir was ashamed.

"It was me," he said. "I was all of those things, not you...I am sorry."

Kiva's expression softened, and she placed a hand on his shoulder. "Don't worry about it big brother. I've only ever wanted to live up to you and Mica."

"And now you've surpassed us both," Mica said.

"Hardly," Kiva argued. "Shadestalkers are born to fight the Sharun...and what good would they *or t*he windwalkers be without stonemelter steel?" she asked, looking at Amir.

"None whatsoever!" Mica agreed.

"Let's go," her father said. "Everyone is waiting."

Everyone? Kiva thought.

She finally made her way out the front door of their home into blinding sunlight. She shielded her eyes as they adjusted, and her ears were met with an immense chorus of high-spirited, raucous, cheering.

Kiva furrowed her brow, squinting. A sea of people stretched out before her, jumping and clapping exuberantly. They were so many, and so tightly packed, that not a patch of ground was visible.

What are they cheering for? she thought.

They cheer for you, Noor answered. Kiva looked up and found the kiraeen flying in big lazy circles, high above the basin.

Me?

Sure enough, Kiva began picking up bits and pieces of what they were saying. They were calling her name!

Kiva felt suddenly uncomfortable. She was more than used to handling criticism and condescending glares, but she had never experienced anything like this.

"Come," her mother said into her ear.

With her parents at either side, and her brothers in tow, Kiva slowly made her way down the stairs leading to the basin floor. There was hardly any sign at all of the chaos that had been visited upon them only a few days before.

It has been over a week, Noor corrected.

A week? Kiva exclaimed. It felt like three days at most.

There were still great piles of sand in corners here and there, but the debris had been cleared, and the sandshields were once again retracted.

As they reached the bottom of the stairs, the exuberant crowd parted to let them through. For Kiva, the experience was surreal. A week ago she had been the object of controversy. An exile, scorned and unwelcome. Now, she was surrounded by smiling, cheering faces. Not only had they accepted her, they *loved* her. Despite the adoration, there was a part of Kiva that remained unsettled. She recalled the blood red flowers and twisting stone spires to the southwest, and wondered what Jonah encountered on the Mujdab Plains. They had kept the Sharun at bay, but at the cost of how many lives? The threat was far from gone.

Kiva and her family continued through the crowd until they reached the same stage on which she'd been exiled. A group of safekeepers were crowded upon it, along with three windwalkers, one of whom was Jonah. The council were present as well, seated on their benches. One bench stood empty—the same that had belonged to Jado. Standing before them all was Lalla Suriel—eldest of the Sahra' mystics—leaning on her cane beside a young man in orange robes.

Kiva swallowed. Her last conversation with this woman had been less than cordial. Nevertheless, she had little choice but to go along with whatever came next. They reached the stairs to the stage, and Kiva's father and brothers held back as her mother helped her onto the platform.

Suriel hobbled over, impatiently waving off the assistance offered by the young man at her side.

Kiva readied herself for the tongue-lashing she would surely receive for disregarding her exile. The old woman approached, and looked up at Kiva with steely gray eyes.

"When you're as old as I am, child, you tend to take much for granted. It is all too easy to forget that wisdom must often be sought, rather than assumed."

Kiva tilted her head, attempting to decipher whether or not she was in trouble.

"A good lesson for myself,"—Suriel's eyes sparkled mischievously—"and all the other *qadim* with one foot in the grave."

Kiva cracked a smile, and Suriel took her arm.

"Thank you, Kivanya," she said with genuine humility. "You've given my grandchildren a chance for full, happy lives. I was gravely mistaken to exile you, and though I do not expect it, I humbly ask your forgiveness."

Kiva was speechless. Judging by the shocked expression of those in earshot, this was not something that happened often, if ever.

"Of course, you have it," Kiva said finally. "Sometimes, it's difficult to believe what is coming, until you've seen it with your own eyes."

"You speak truth, Kivanya Fariq. And now we have all seen the terrifying power of the threat we must face. Come, our people await."

They walked together toward the front of the stage. Suriel hobbled, hunched over on her cane, and Kiva walked gingerly in small, shuffling steps.

"We must look quite the pair," Kiva said.

Suriel barked a laugh. "And still tougher than any man in the crowd!"

A great cheer erupted as they reached the center of the

stage. Kiva looked out over the staggering mass of people before her. Surely every last Sahra' stood in attendance.

Suriel held up her hand for quiet, and received it a moment later.

"Someone wise once said to me that it is sometimes difficult to believe what is coming, unless seen with one's own eyes. Often, those with the courage to speak out risk hostility, and ostracism. Why is this?" she asked rhetorically. "It is because we do not *want* to believe. Surely, this was true for myself." Suriel paused, gathering her thoughts.

"Kivanya Fariq, your exile is hereby annulled. Should you choose to forgive us, we would be honored to have you among us once more."

The crowd cheered wildly, in obvious agreement with Suriel's statement. After several seconds, she once again raised a palm to quiet them so that Kiva could speak.

Kiva wiped the sweat in her palms on her tunic. "I... thank you," she said.

"Well?" Suriel asked. "Would you count yourself among the Sahra' once more?"

"Yes!" Kiva called out, and the crowd cheered once again.

"It is done!" Suriel shouted. She then turned to Kiva. "Well done, child."

Suriel gestured for her to stand aside. "Now, Councilman Daivari would speak."

Daivari stood from his seat on the bench, and walked past the safekeepers who stood to his left, and the three windwalkers to his right. Kiva later learned that the rest of the windwalker sect had survived the storm by taking shelter.

Jonah and these two flew *through* it, in order to provide aid to the basin.

Kiva's eyes met Jonah's, and they shared a smile.

"The Sharun have returned," Daivari's voice held such vehemence, that the crowd grew silent. "Many, if not all of you have seen with your own eyes what this means. Those of you who haven't seen, have surely heard. It has been three hundred years since any have laid eyes upon them. Now, we have seen first hand the fury, and the power they wield. But we have also seen the strength and the courage of our people!"

The mass of people before him began to murmur, giving the occasional shout.

"The safekeepers who managed to break free and fight!" Davari called out with his powerful voice, gesturing to them. The crowd was once again cheering loudly.

"The windwalkers, who assailed the sandshades from above!"

More cheers came, and Kiva heard Jonah's name amongst the yelling.

"And finally," he said, waiting for the cheering to subside, "For the one among us who refused to be what she was told to be. Whose strength of will and unwavering purpose," he surveyed the crowd, "are the reason so many of us remain alive today."

Kiva blushed. This was far more than she felt she deserved. Looking out at the faces in the crowd, she began to understand that Daivari's words were not meant to flatter her. They were meant to bring hope to their people.

"I speak of Kivanya Fariq, of the windwalker sect," he said with finality.

Kiva felt a powerful sense of pride. *The windwalker sect.*

The crowd was loud before, but now it had grown deafening.

Noor, Kiva thought. *This is your victory as much as mine.*

A great screech pierced the air, and many in the crowd turned their faces up to watch and cheer, as Noor performed a series of impressive aerobatics.

Daivari held up his hands, signaling quiet.

"The council is in agreement: this must be the last time the Sharun catch us off guard. Windwalker patrols will be doubled, shadestalker strike parties will bring the fight to the enemy, and safekeepers will ensure that every inch of Sahra' territory is secure.

"Unfortunately, this simply cannot be achieved with sect numbers what they are. Therefore, the council has agreed upon the need for new sects, mirroring those of the windwalker, shadestalker, and safekeeper sects. They will maintain the same honors, respects, and challenges, only they will be led by Lallas, and remain exclusive to female challengers."

The crowd's reaction to this news was mixed. The majority of the cheering came from the women of the basin, but still, there were no vocal objections. Kiva's mother had told her the new sects were coming, but the announcement was still striking to witness. She wondered to herself if it mattered whether progress stemmed from conviction, or from a practical need for survival.

"And now," Daivari spoke, "Let us celebrate the strength and prowess of our warriors!" The crowd again began cheering in earnest. "Let us show the Sharun, that nothing can break the Sahra' spirit!"

With his final words, music and drumming burst out from the crowd. The celebration had officially begun. Kiva was nearly mobbed by the safekeepers. Each of them wanting to greet her and shake her hand. They asked her questions about Noor, and expressed their wonder at her kiraeen's ferocity.

She was also visited by the council, who congratulated her on her accomplishments. Strangely, some of them even treated her as if *she* were the authority. The only one not to approach her was Councilman Elam, who had vanished from the stage soon after Daivari's speech.

At last, it was time for Kiva to greet her fellow windwalkers. Jonah allowed the other two to approach first, and Kiva spoke with them as quickly as possible, without being rude. They congratulated her, suggesting she lead the new sister-sect, before joining the jubilant throngs.

Finally, she thought. It was time to greet the one person in the basin she desired to see over all others. He stepped forward and took her hands. They shared a look, then stole off together, seeking somewhere private. It proved nearly impossible, until Kiva was gifted a beautiful blue and gold headscarf by a grateful stranger in the crowd. She wrapped her head, covering her face with it, and they were able to slip away.

They discovered an entryway with a smashed and broken door, and slipped inside. Judging by the crates and shelving, it had been used by a merchant for storage. No sooner had they closed the broken door, than Kiva felt Jonah's hand gently caressing her face. His lips pressed against hers, tenderly at first, then with growing passion. Kiva's blood was a firestorm. It threatened to overwhelm her at any moment.

She gently drew back, smiling. There was still something she needed to know. "You said that once a windwalker is bonded, there is little room for much else...that you were fine with being alone."

Jonah took a deep breath. "You're right, I did say that, didn't I?" He ran a hand through his hair. "Before you, I even believed it...Listen Kiva, ever since I became a windwalker, I always just assumed it would be *Zakai and Jonah* to the end. I had convinced myself I was better off alone...then you came along and everything changed." Jonah furrowed his brow, searching for the right words, then met her eyes. "Kivanya, you're incredible."

Kiva looked at him with skepticism.

"It's true!" he insisted. "Even Zakai thinks so." Jonah placed his hands on her arms. "Not only did you forgive the entire basin for what they did to you, but you risked your life to protect them."

"They are my people," Kiva said plainly. The fact that she would protect them, whether or not they wanted her around, was simply a given.

"You are smart, caring, beautiful, fearless..."

Kiva smiled, raising an eyebrow. She rather liked it when he was the one putting himself out there, for a change.

"I used to think the bond was enough," Jonah continued, "I was wrong."

Kiva met his eyes in the dim light, and was left with no doubt as to his sincerity. She understood exactly what he meant. Her bond with Noor was powerful and ever-present. They shared preferences, desires, emotions...their personalities had even begun to meld. She understood how it could seem overwhelming, bringing love into the picture. Yet even with the intimate connection she shared with her kiraeen, her heart still yearned to be close to Jonah. It was so powerful an emotion, that even Noor was coming around to the idea.

"And back in Noor's den?" she asked. "When I kissed you?" Kiva recalled the hesitant look on his face.

"I guess…I was scared," he admitted, casting his eyes downward. "When my father left, I lost the only person I really cared about…it's hard to come back from something like that."

"But you have," Kiva looked up at him, drawing his gaze.

"Yeah," he said, wearing the same small smile that drove her crazy. "I guess I have."

"You guess?" she asked in mock outrage.

"Well that, and Zakai would drop me from a thousand feet if I let you slip away…he's quite possibly your second biggest fan."

"Oh yeah?" she asked. "Who's the first?"

He answered her with another kiss, and nothing more was said between them for a very long time.

END OF BOOK ONE

Dear reader

Thank you for reading Windwalker. It really is very much appreciated. If you enjoyed it, I'd be extremely grateful if you could leave a short review on Amazon.

Thank you again.

H.G.

Books by H.G. Chambers

WINDWALKER SERIES

Windwalker: Forbidden Flight
Windwalker: Relic of the Dead

THE AETERNUM CHRONICLES

Recreance (Book 1)
Vigilance (Book 2)
Defiance (Book 3)

EXTRAS

Want more from this author?
Sign up for the H.G. Chambers reader group, and receive once a month updates on new releases, as well as exclusive behind the scenes content, including concept art, deleted scenes, character bios, and more!

Sign up at www.hgchambers.com

Meet the Author

Harold George Chambers is an award winning fantasy science fiction writer. He's also a dad, a helicopter pilot, web designer, musician, and a huge board game nerd. Inspired by the great fantasy sci-fi authors of the past and present, Harold published *Recreance*, the first book of The Aeternum Chronicles, in 2017. The story continues with *Vigilance*, released early 2018. Harold makes his home in a small Canadian town on Vancouver Island with his wife and four-year-old son. To learn more about him, visit www.hgchambers.com.

Introducing

If you enjoyed
WINDWALKER: Forbidden Flight,
you won't want to miss

WINDWALKER: Relic of the Dead

*Book two of the Windwalker Series
by H.G. Chambers*

THE VALLEY

Quiet! You're going to draw their attention, Kiva scolded.

Let it be drawn then, Noor snapped. *I'm tired of hiding like a frightened sand hare.*

Despite her protestations, Noor remained crouched and unmoving.

It's just until we have the advantage, Kiva sent the thought to Noor. *Even now, the shadestalkers are moving into position.*

Lying flat on her belly against the rock, Kiva shifted slightly, daring to raise her head above the ridge to get a better look at the desert valley below. It was a sheer drop, hundreds of feet down to the sandy floor. Behind Kiva, Noor was crouched low, resting on the angled joints at the leading edges of her broad, black-feathered wings. She snapped her beak, and Kiva turned with an admonishing glare. The kiraeen met her level gaze, long tail whipping back and forth along the ground.

Behave, Kiva warned. *None of the others are complaining.* She glanced back at the two additional windwalkers, lying low beside their crouched kiraeen.

Males, Noor spat, as if that explained everything.

Kiva turned her attention back to the long valley, where a column of seventy-three sharun warriors, four to five abreast, were shambling their way through.

Ever since the attack on Madina Basin, the sharun had been cropping up everywhere. Kiva was unsure whether they simply wandered the Miralaja looking for Sahra' to kill, or if they had some greater collective purpose. Either way, they'd become an ever-present danger.

Even from high above, Kiva could make out the twisted, animalistic masks and armor they wore. So far she'd counted fifteen varieties, though she was unable to discern any difference beyond appearance. They moved like soldiers weary from sun-sickness, but she knew from experience how they would instantly stir into a frenzy at the smell of blood.

If not for Noor's battle lust surging across the bond into Kiva's mind, she'd have been trembling like a leaf. Sharun warriors fought and killed without remorse or hesitation. They possessed inhuman strength, experienced no pain, and could survive wounds that would kill even the strongest Sahra' warrior. Cut off a limb, and it simply grew back. Cut off their heads and they'd be down for a time, but unless the crystals of their eyes were destroyed, they'd rise up once more as if nothing had happened.

Fortunately, the newly risen threat had galvanized the people of the basin. Sects that once worked alone were now coordinating to protect their home. Because of this, the windwalkers would not be facing the current threat alone. Across the valley on another ridge to the north was a war party of shadestalkers—the Sahra's most elite battle sect, trained in secret to strike at the sharun with unyielding force and needle-point precision. Lying in wait among them, was Kiva's brother, Mica.

Kiva's muscles twitched in anticipation. It had been early

morning when she first spotted the sharun from Noor's back, high above. Being too large a force to take by themselves, she and Noor had sped back to Madina Basin for support. By the time they'd devised a plan with the shadestalkers and traveled to this place, the sun was well on its journey westward.

The sharun slowly continued down the sandy desert valley, their grunts and growls echoing off its rocky walls. The wait was nearly over.

A flicker in her peripheral drew her attention.

What is it? Noor asked.

I thought I saw something at the end of the column. Probably just a mirage from the heat...Get ready.

Kiva's grip on the spear lying beside her tightened as the sharun continued moving, oblivious to the trap awaiting them.

One of the shadestalkers on the opposite ridge raised his fist.

Kiva's heart thudded audibly, sending vibrations through her entire body. She and Noor had dispatched several small parties of three or four sharun warriors, but this was by far the biggest group she'd come across since the attack on Madina Basin.

She turned to the two windwalkers behind her and raised her eyebrows. They nodded, and Kiva raised her fist into the sky, signaling their readiness. She felt Noor's consciousness, coiled and compressed like a spring, ready to burst.

So far, everything was going according to plan. By attacking the sharun column from the sides, they would divide their enemy's forces into smaller, more manageable groups.

From there, they would be isolated and killed well before they reached the basin.

The shadestalker across the valley drew his fist down, and Kiva did the same. She sprung to her feet, and leapt from the sheer ridge into open air, arms and legs spread wide. In seconds Noor was streaking down toward her. The two had grown fully attuned to each other, both knowing what the other would do before she did it.

Wind whipped violently at Kiva's clothing as she fell, yet her vision was undisturbed—a welcome benefit of the bond she'd forged with Noor. Sensing her approach, Kiva positioned herself to grasp the kiraeen's harness. In the next instant, Noor's dark form appeared below, matching Kiva's descent. With spear in hand, the windwalker settled onto Noor's back, and braced for the force of pulling up from the dive.

You are aware that you lack the feathers for flight? Noor asked.

That's why I have you, Kiva answered with an impish grin.

A quick glance back up the ridge revealed the other windwalkers and their kiraeen also taking flight.

Noor shrieked a deafening battle cry as they sped toward the sharun, who were only just beginning to turn and take notice. Chills ran across Kiva's skin at the ferocity of Noor's cry, and she almost felt pity for the landbound sharun.

Across the valley, the shadestalkers were spilling down over the far ridge, sprinting silently with weapons drawn.

She and Noor began to level out, flying low over the ground at great speed. They were aimed at the very middle of the long column, intent on dividing it in two. Kiva was tucked low against Noor's back, allowing for as much speed as possible.

Almost, Kiva thought, watching as a few of the sharun wedged the butt of their spears in the sand, angling upward.

Now!

Kiva and Noor simultaneously pulled back. Thrusting Noor's powerful legs forward. They crashed into the sharun column with incredible force. Spears snapped, and Noor's victims went flying through the air. Their bodies exploded into clouds of sand upon impact with the far slope of the valley. Kiva made a mental note of their location—they'd be reformed in a matter of minutes if no one destroyed the small crystals that gave them life.

Noor pumped her powerful wings, climbing skyward as the other windwalkers crashed into the column on either side of her attack, dividing it further.

As she wheeled around for another strike, Kiva watched for the shadestalkers. The majority were colliding with the broken column, while another small group quickly sprinted to where the sharun had fallen moments ago. They drew spiked hammers—broad and flat on one side—and began crushing the sharun crystals, preventing their regeneration. Kiva swelled with pride at seeing the weapons her father had designed.

She scanned the battle, searching for her next target, when she again noticed something strange at the rear of the column—a place where the sand seemed to shimmer and distort.

Kiva watched with keen eyes, and it soon became clear.

There was a sharun there, somehow camouflaged against the sand. It held a long staff, which it was waving in large circles overhead. At that moment, a great inverted funnel of sand began swirling up before it.

What is it doing? Kiva asked, but the answer soon became clear.

Sharun titan. Noor confirmed. *Two of them.*

Two? Where? Kiva asked, peering ahead.

The other end of the column.

Kiva turned upon Noor's back. Her chest tightened as she realized it wasn't the sharun who were trapped, but her own people.

The sharun with the staff, Kiva thought, *it's summoning the titans. We have to stop it!*

Noor's wings were already tucked against her body as she dove for the target.

Up ahead, the swirling sand coalesced into a massive form before the near-invisible sharun. In seconds it was whole—a towering creature covered in large, smooth segments. Its long tail curled up behind, as two razor-sharp claws solidified at the ends of segmented limbs on either side of its head.

Kiva glanced back and saw another forming at the opposite end.

Al'ama, she cursed.

The shade before her darkened to a glossy black, and the clusters of crystals that served as its eyes began pulsing in deep purple hues.

We cannot reach the summoner, Noor warned.

Right, she thought. *We need to protect the shadestalkers.*

She and Noor pulled into a vertical climb just as the titan's tail flew past. It smashed into the ground, sending a cloud of sand and dust into the air.

I have an idea, Kiva thought. She relayed the plan to Noor.

You are sure? Noor asked... *The claws...*

I am, Kiva responded, and they changed course.

The massive scorpion was moving, heedlessly crushing its own sharun under segmented legs as it charged the shadestalkers.

Faster, Kiva urged. Noor's powerful wings beat against the wind.

Below, a bloodcurdling scream was cut short by a loud *clack*.

Kiva's jaw tightened. One of her people had fallen. In that instant the thrill of combat within her was replaced by grim determination.

Noor swooped high into the air, then gracefully arced into a dive aimed at the titan's right flank. They had no chance of overpowering a creature so large, and thus had to rely on their considerable speed and agility.

There was another loud *clack* as a pair of serrated claws snapped shut nearby, catching only air.

Kiva braced as Noor spread her wings and thrust out her rear talons. They crash-landed onto the hardshell back of the titan, skidding several feet before coming to a stop. Kiva shook her head, and leapt off Noor's back. The kiraeen quickly recovered and launched herself into the air. The scorpion bucked under Kiva, who lowered her body in an effort to keep her footing. She stabbed her spear down against its carapace in frustration, but the steel tip clanked harmlessly off the scorpion's shell.

The gigantic insect's body steadied for a moment, its attention drawn by a flying spear from a shadestalker warrior. Kiva took full advantage of the distraction and scurried toward the head, keeping low to maintain balance. She clenched the fist of her left hand, tightening her grip on the broad steel plate fitted across her knuckles—another of her father's innovations.

Soon she would crush the crystals that gave it life, and reduce this monster to a pile of sand. The titan scorpion raised its claws. She would soon be in range of both, if she wasn't already.

Noor carved a sharp path through the air, diving toward the front of the massive arthropod. She streaked past its deadly pincers but they clacked shut empty, unable to match the kiraeen's speed. Kiva reached the head and leapt into the air, raising her steel-plated fist. She brought it crashing down onto one of the scorpion's eye clusters, shattering a few of the crystals embedded there.

It *hissed* as the bottom half of one pincer sloughed off, turning it into a giant serrated club. The other, still whole, struck out with unexpected speed. Kiva sprung back, away from the head, hoping she was out of range. The pincer *clacked* shut mere inches behind her.

Noor was again streaking down, attempting to draw the titan's attention. A shadow passed over Kiva. She looked up to see the tip of the scorpion's curved tail hovering directly above.

Get ready, she thought, and Noor acknowledged.

With the scorpion's pincers now targeting Noor, Kiva

again sprung for the head. This time she stopped dead center between the eye clusters. With both hands wrapped tightly around her spear, she stabbed it down with force repeatedly, the tip clanking harmlessly off the carapace.

She looked up as the scorpion tail blocked out the sun, casting her in shadow.

"Harab alan!" Kiva shouted the command for the treacherous escape maneuver.

She leapt into the air, spreading her arms wide. Noor streaked toward her, rear legs reaching low with talons wide.

The curving tail of the colossal scorpion descended with terrifying speed.

Kiva flexed her shoulders as Noor's talons closed around her biceps. She was yanked forward, buffeted by the wind of the tail's spiked tip rushing past.

There was a loud *crunch*, as the tail smashed into the scorpion's head where Kiva had stood. She looked back, watching as the entire creature changed from black to sandy brown. The tail began to disintegrate, spreading down to the body and legs until it was nothing more than a large pile of sand.

Noor climbed, Kiva's arms still held tightly in her talons. Once high enough, the kiraeen released her rider. Kiva spread her arms and legs wide, controlling her fall. Noor looped backwards, diving with great speed. She soon caught up, matching Kiva's descent, then glided beneath her with pinpoint accuracy. Kiva once again settled onto Noor's back, and they prepared to resume their attack.

Kiva scanned toward the far end of the column to find the other two windwalker kiraeen harrying the scorpion as the shadestalkers assaulted its eyes. The tail had disintegrated away, and its pincers were reduced to a pair of serrated bludgeons. It appeared the remaining sharun warriors had been dispatched, though there was still the possibility of more rising.

With the second scorpion well in hand, Kiva turned her attention to the sharun responsible for summoning the colossal beasts.

Instead of a camouflaged figure, her eyes found a darkened whirlwind of sand, retreating away down the valley with incredible speed.

She glanced back one last time, then urged Noor to follow.

Noor expressed the slightest hesitation before speeding after the fleeing whirlwind. She pumped her wings, each sweep thrusting them forward with greater speed.

We're gaining on it, Kiva thought.

As they sped away from the main battle, the walls of the valley changed from rocky stone to towering dunes of sand. Before long they had nearly caught up with the sharun summoner.

Suddenly the whirlwind spun itself out, revealing a figure standing defiant atop a narrow hill of sand in the center of the valley. Unlike the other crudely masked sharun, this one bore an elaborate, black and golden jawless jackal mask, its two ears pointed back and up. Orange light from the setting sun glinted off the thin layered strips of white and gold armor on its shoulders, chest, and legs. It raised a gold staff with the head of a cobra.

Kiva met its eyes, and a chill ran through her bones at the intelligence there. She gripped her spear, both windwalker and kiraeen focused to a razor's edge. Lifting her weapon, Kiva prepared to throw.

"*Munfasil*" the sharun's deep, raspy voice echoed in Kiva's head.

Kiva gasped in shock, reeling as if struck.

What is happening?

Something was wrong. *Very* wrong.

With dawning horror she realized that Noor's familiar presence in the corner of her mind had abruptly vanished.

WINDWALKER: Relic of the Dead

Book two of the Windwalker Series

Get it today on Amazon

ACKNOWLEDGMENTS

My sincerest thanks to everyone who has been a part of this story. This includes my loving wife, Melanie, who provided invaluable insight into how a young woman would think and react. A huge thank you to Jane Tucker, for your brilliant suggestions, and masterful editing. Lastly, thanks to all of you for reading this book. Your support is what allows me to keep writing.

Newsletter

Thank you for reading Windwalker!

Would you like access to exclusive content, including concept art, deleted scenes, character bios, and more? Sign up for the H.G. Chambers monthly newsletter, and all of this can be yours! You'll also be the first to hear about new releases.

Sign up at www.hgchambers.com

Manufactured by Amazon.ca
Bolton, ON